Small Medium at Large

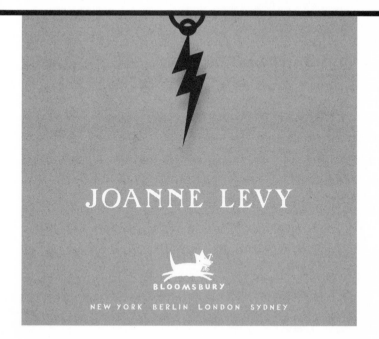

Small Medium at Large

JOANNE LEVY

BLOOMSBURY

NEW YORK BERLIN LONDON SYDNEY

First published in the United States of America in July 2012
by Bloomsbury Books for Young Readers
www.bloomsburykids.com

For information about permission to reproduce selections from this book, write to
Permissions, Bloomsbury BFYR, 175 Fifth Avenue, New York, New York 10010

Library of Congress Cataloging-in-Publication Data
Levy, Joanne.
Small medium at large / by Joanne Levy. — 1st U.S. ed.
p.   cm.
Summary: After being hit by lightning, twelve-year-old Lilah, who has a crush on classmate
Andrew Finkel, discovers that she can communicate with dead people, including her
grandmother, who wants Lilah to find a new wife for Lilah's divorced father.
ISBN 978-1-59990-836-6
[1. Mediums—Fiction. 2. Dating (Interpersonal relations)—Fiction. 3. Jews—
United States—Fiction.] I. Title.
PZ7.L58323Sm 2012   [Fic]—dc22   2011034463

Book design by Donna Mark
Typeset by Westchester Book Composition
Printed in the U.S.A. by Quad/Graphics, Fairfield, Pennsylvania
2 4 6 8 10 9 7 5 3 1

All papers used by Bloomsbury Publishing, Inc., are natural, recyclable products
made from wood grown in well-managed forests. The manufacturing processes
conform to the environmental regulations of the country of origin.

For Deke,
who never, ever doubted

Small Medium at Large

CHAPTER 1

Despite the suffocating mid-May heat and the nonbreathable fabric of my lavender polyester dress, it was shaping up to be a very good day.

As a matter of fact, the entire week leading up to my mother's wedding had been *exceptionally* good. Mom was finally marrying her boyfriend, Stan, which was great, since he was a nice guy and didn't try to replace my dad in *my* life, and as a bridesmaid, I had received an iPod (the awesome kind that holds a gazillion songs) as a wedding party thank-you gift.

The only person not happy about the nuptials was my poor dad, who hadn't done anything to get back out there since the divorce. Nothing. Like, not one date or even a profile on an online dating site.

He was pretty deep in denial, but this wedding was the final nail in the coffin of his marriage. But more about him later.

So now that the ceremony was over, the brunch had been eaten, and a few crazy individuals were sweating it up on the dance floor under the big white tent, my best friend, Alex, and I sat at a table sipping our iced teas, listening to the band.

"Ugh, I can't believe anyone would want to play a wedding gig," Alex said.

I snorted. "We haven't even started our band yet, and already you're too good for weddings?"

"Uh, yeah. No weddings or bar mitzvahs for us, my dear Lilah. We're going big time."

I had my doubts, since we could barely play, still needed instruments, and hadn't even had our own bat mitzvahs yet, *and* so far it was only the two of us. Our dreams of having a band were still just that: dreams.

"You've got quite an inflamed ego for someone who doesn't even own her own guitar."

Alex held the cool glass up to her forehead and rolled it back and forth. It was hard to believe it was only May.

"We're going to be huge. And the guys are going to be all over us. You watch. We will get to choose our boyfriends from the cream of the crop."

That's one thing you probably need to know about Alex: she's boy crazy. And I mean CRAZY. She has a crush on a new guy almost every day. I'm more the consistent type: I've been crushing all over Andrew Finkel since the first day of seventh grade, when he showed up at our school. He barely knew I was alive, but in the nine months he'd been in our class, I'd become fairly sure he would be the perfect boyfriend and the perfect guy to go to the seventh-grade dance with. Not that he would ever ask me in a million years, but still, a girl can dream, right? Andrew had shaggy brown hair and emerald-green eyes. Perfect. And he was really nice, which is also very important in a potential boyfriend.

"Lilah!"

I stopped thinking about Andrew and turned toward my friend. "What?"

"I asked what you thought of *him*." She nodded toward the dessert table, keeping her eyes on me.

I slowly turned my head to find the object of her inquiry. It was my cousin Ira. "He's eighteen, Alex."

"Yes, but when he's forty-eight, I'll be forty-two, and by then it won't matter."

"Whatever. I really think . . . uh-oh." I stopped midsentence because my aunt Rosie was making a beeline for our table.

Alex followed my eyes and groaned when she saw my aunt.

Two seconds later, she was looming over us.

"Hi, Aunt Rosie," I said. "You remember Alex?"

She nodded politely at my friend. "Nice to see you, Alexandra."

Alex, who loathed being called by her full name, mumbled something in return.

Aunt Rosie quickly turned back to me. Without warning, she grabbed my chin tightly in her hand, holding my gaze with her amber eyes. "Everything going okay, Delilah?"

Maybe a little backstory on Aunt Rosie is required. She and Mom are sisters, but sharing a little DNA from their parents is where the similarities end. Mom's a money-motivated financial adviser for one of the big banks. Rosie's a true bohemian chick who makes jewelry in her one-bedroom apartment and sells it at a farmers' market (and sometimes, if sales aren't great and she ends up with a surplus, on Etsy, thanks to yours truly). She always smells like sandalwood incense and even wore a peasant skirt and Birkenstocks to the wedding, much to my mother's horror.

Anyway, there she was, holding my face and staring at me while she waited for my answer.

"Yeah, I'm fine, Aunt Rosie."

She frowned, but let go of my chin. "I see something."

I grabbed the compact out of my tiny clutch purse and held it up to my face. "What? Do I have food on my face? Am I breaking out or something? I knew I shouldn't have eaten all that cake at the rehearsal—"

"No, Delilah, I don't see a blemish on your face, but a rift in your aura. Something big is coming for you."

See what I mean?

"I'm fine, Aunt Rosie, really, maybe it's just . . ." I was going to say the stress of the wedding or my period was coming, but before I could finish, she squealed and flittered off, having suddenly noticed the dessert table.

"What a kook," Alex said. Exactly what I had just been thinking.

I watched my aunt load up a plate with sweets and fruit and then head over to the bar for what undoubtedly was not her first glass of champagne. She was weird, but totally harmless, and usually a good source of amusement. I shrugged it off, not paying much attention to what she had said.

"Lilah?"

I turned toward my friend. "What?"

"Guy at the chocolate fountain."

As inconspicuously as I could, I turned to look.

Jason, Stan's son and my new stepbrother, was holding a handful of fruit under the chocolate drizzle. He may as well have put his mouth under the nozzle.

"Gross," I said. "That's Stan's son."

Alex was practically drooling as she gawked at him. "I know. He's cute."

I clucked my tongue. "He's disgusting."

"So? What's a few germs between friends?"

"You're hopeless."

She shrugged and went back to ogling Jason.

Sipping my tea, I scanned the crowd, trying to find my mom. She and Stan were at table eight, holding hands and talking to their guests. They were both smiling and laughing, having a great time. My heart swelled a little at how happy Mom obviously was.

She and Stan had met at the supermarket; I'd even been there to witness it. They were at the deli counter, Mom for shaved turkey and Stan for roast beef. As they waited for their numbers to be called, they struck up a conversation about olives. It was weird, because I still can't believe anyone likes olives, but there they were talking about pimentos and Kalamatas versus green olives or whatever it is one discusses when talking about olives. (I'll be honest and tell you I really wasn't listening.) But I guess, after all, it wasn't really about olives, because the very next

Friday night they went on a date, and it turned out they didn't even eat any olives (I asked when Mom got home).

But as I watched them now, it made me think of my dad, who had no one to discuss olives or lunch meats with, other than me. He was lonely, and I think until very recently (like when he dropped me off at the synagogue that very morning) he actually thought there was a chance Mom would still be coming back.

Um, no.

And just because he still insisted on wearing his wedding band didn't mean he was still married.

It was really sad. But what could I do?

I sipped the last of my tea and turned to Alex. "Want to dance or something?"

She shook her head. "Too hot."

I nodded. It really was hot. The people on the dance floor were nuts. But they seemed to be enjoying themselves. The music was okay, but it was all songs I didn't recognize; they were obviously old-school tunes that the adults could dance to.

"So Lilah, when do you think we'll get out of here?"

"Dad's picking us up at four thirty."

Alex sighed but pushed herself up off her chair. "If I'm gonna be stuck here another two hours,

I'm gonna need to rehydrate. You want another drink?"

I nodded. "Yes, please."

"Lilah!" Mom said, appearing at our table. "Are you having a good time?"

"Of course! And may I say once again, you are a breathtaking bride!" (These are the kinds of things you must say to the bride, whether or not she's your mother.)

Her big smile told me I was right on the money. "Thanks, hon."

"And you look fetching, too, Stan."

He nodded politely, but I could tell from his eyes that he appreciated the compliment. Stan is a guy of few words. Which is okay because my mom is a woman of many.

"We're getting ready to go soon, Lilah, but we wanted to thank you again for being my bridesmaid and for helping out with the wedding."

"You're welcome," I said. "You two seem very happy."

Mom smiled. "Thanks, honey." Then, her eyes got all glassy. "I'm going to miss you soooooo much."

Of course, then *my* eyes filled up. I was going to miss Mom, too. Even though I live with Dad in the house I've always lived in, it was going to be hard not to see Mom for the month that she and Stan would be touring Europe on their honeymoon. I usually slept over at her house at least once a weekend, and we had lots of shopping days and movie nights, so I was definitely going to notice her not being around for thirty whole days. "I'll miss you, too, Mom. Make sure you guys take lots of pictures and you can e-mail me every day."

Of course Mom would e-mail. She was so attached to e-mail that she almost made her BlackBerry a bridesmaid (I'm kidding).

But still, e-mail wouldn't be the same.

"Where's your bouquet?" she asked suddenly.

I looked around the table, realizing I hadn't seen it in a while. My heart skipped in panic because I had big plans to dry the flowers and make them into a nice potpourri to give to Mom on her next birthday.

"I think you left it in the limo," Alex said.

"Oh! That's right!" I'd been so excited about my first ride in a limo with Mom and Stan from the synagogue to the reception that I left my bouquet on the seat.

I jumped out of my chair. "I'll be right back; I want to go get it before you leave."

Stan looked at his watch. "We'd better get going, Maggie," he said to my mom.

She nodded. "I just need to thank the rabbi."

I threw myself at my mom and gave her a big hug. "Congratulations, Mom. I'm really happy for you."

She squeezed me tight. "Thanks, honey. I'll e-mail you every day, I promise."

I couldn't help but cry a little, but since Mom had tears in her eyes, too, I figured it was okay. Before we really messed up our faces, I turned and headed toward the limo to get my bouquet.

There was a long winding path that would take me to the parking lot, but it was faster to cut across the lawn, so I jogged across the grass as best I could in my heels.

The sky was darkening and a bunch of clouds had rolled in—maybe a storm was coming. Even though I was practically melting from the heat, I sped up my pace, not wanting to get stuck in a shower.

The limo driver opened the door so I could get my bouquet, which was very nice of him. I noticed there was a bottle of wine chilling in a bucket of ice, which was a really classy way to travel, if you ask me. I thanked the man, who tipped his hat at me. Then I jogged back to the tent, bouquet in hand.

I got under the canopy and held on to the support pole as I scraped the mud off my shoes on the edge of the temporary floor.

Suddenly, a shiver ran through me and all the little hairs on my arms stood on end, freaking me out a little. A rumble seemed to vibrate through the earth. I leaned out of the tent and looked up into the dark sky.

There was a sudden, deafening *snap!*

And then everything went dark.

CHAPTER 2

I opened my eyes, unsure where I was. But I quickly closed them against the assault of the superbright lights in the room. I still didn't know where I was, but I was pretty sure I wasn't at home in my own bed, since my room couldn't possibly be that bright without the addition of about twenty sunlamps.

"She's awake, thank goodness," I heard a distant but familiar voice say.

Slowly prying my lids open, I allowed in tiny bits of light at a time. I quickly figured out I was in a hospital room. *My* hospital room, as in I was the person lying on a bed in the middle of it.

Wow, that's messed up. One minute you're scraping crud off your shoe, the next you're waking up in a hospital room.

"Oh!" Mom, still in her wedding gown, jumped

up from a chair in the corner and put her hand on my forehead. "She doesn't seem to have a fever."

Dad was on the other side of the bed looking down at me, a very concerned expression on his face.

"Wha . . . ," I croaked, my throat so dry the words wouldn't come out. Mindful of the IV line running into my arm, I mimed a drink and pointed at my neck.

"I'll go get the nurse." Dad disappeared, hopefully to also get me a glass of water.

"Just take it easy, honey." Mom stroked my cheek with her left hand, the one that now sported her engagement ring and wedding band. If she was here and still wearing her wedding gown, it meant . . . oh, crap.

I forced some saliva into my mouth and swallowed. "Honeymoon?" I managed, looking over at Stan who was standing at the back of the room by the window, still wearing his tux, although the bow tie was hanging loose at his neck.

Weird, it was probably the first time my parents had been in the same room since Mom had brought Stan over to tell Dad they were getting married. *That* had not been a good day either.

"Oh, honey, we're not going anywhere. We need to make sure you're okay."

"What happened?" I forced out, despite the fire in my throat.

Dad returned to the room, thankfully with a paper cup, just in time to answer my question. "You were hit by lightning." He held the straw up to my lips, and I sucked down the cool water.

Wait a minute, I thought as his words sunk in. *I was hit by* lightning?

I stared at Dad.

He nodded. "Really."

I turned and looked at my mom. "I'm sorry about your honeymoon."

"She'll get over it. She's concerned about you," someone, a woman, said. My mom's lips weren't moving, so I swiveled my head around; there were no other women in the room.

"What did you say?" I asked Mom.

"*She* didn't say it. *I* did. Oy, Lilah."

I was looking at my mom, and there were no words coming out of her mouth, yet a female was speaking to me.

Okay, what's going on? I was clearly losing it.

"It's me."

I turned to look at the other side of the room where the voice seemed to be coming from. Just my dad over there.

"No. It's *me*." The voice became more insistent, frustrated.

I looked back at Mom. "Have I had any medicine?"

She shook her head.

"Can I have some, please?"

"I guess you can't see me," the voice said. "But I'm here. Lilah, it's *me*, your grandmother, Dora."

HUH?

I looked back at Dad. "Do you hear her?"

"Who?"

"Bubby Dora?" Surely he'd be able to hear his own mother's voice.

Dad's forehead wrinkled up as he grabbed my hand and squeezed it. "Lilah, your grandmother's been gone for four years." He looked up at Mom. "Maybe the nurse can get her something to help her sleep."

Good idea.

"You don't need any medicine," Bubby Dora said. "Tell your father not to be so closed-minded. He had no imagination as a child. I see he's gotten no better since I died. *Tsk.*"

Tears sprang to my eyes as I felt my sanity slip away. Thankfully, the nurse and her sleep-inducing pills were right behind.

"Are you awake? I think we need to talk." The voice was as loud as if there was a person speaking right next to me. I looked around the room, but despite the restorative sleep, I was still hearing things.

"You're not hearing things. Well, you are, but it's me you're hearing, your bubby."

"Bubby?" I whispered into the dimness. "What happened to me?"

"Well, you were hit by lightn—"

"No," I interrupted. "What happened to me that I can hear you? Are you really there, or am I crazy?"

"I'm here. You're not crazy."

I took a deep breath. "So can you explain why I can hear you now?"

"It must have been the lightning doing something to your wiring. I can't explain it, but I felt it when you were hit."

"Were you there?" It felt surreal talking to a dis-embodied voice, but I had so many questions. And it sure sounded like my late grandmother. And even if I was crazy, it was kind of comforting talking to her.

"I wasn't able to attend the wedding, unfortu-nately, but when the lightning hit you, it was like someone switched on a radio and I was tuned to your channel. That's the best way I can describe it."

"Huh."

"But I'm glad it happened," she said.

Personally, I wasn't so sure. It was very weird. "What's it like to be dead? And what were you doing that you can be here but you couldn't come to Mom's wedding?"

There was a very long pause. So long, I began to think she was gone, when she suddenly said, "I'm sorry, but I can't tell you."

"Oh," I said, a little disappointed. I mean, what's the use of talking to dead people if they can't tell you about being dead?

"Sorry, Lilah, I just can't. But as you can probably tell, I'm doing okay. That's all you really need to know."

I guess *that* was of some comfort. I smoothed the blanket around me and looked out the window, trying to gauge what time it was. Had to be late, the hospital seemed so quiet.

"So now what?" I said. Was my dead grandmother going to become a 24/7 fixture in my life?

"I need you to help me."

My dead grandmother needed my help? For what? Was there some old mah-jongg crony of hers she needed help haunting?

"No, nothing like that," she said. And even though it had been four years since she'd died, I could picture her standing there with her hands on her hips while she read my mind.

"Wait a minute, you can read my mind?"

"No, but I could tell by the look on your face you were thinking something awful."

"I don't know, I thought maybe you wanted

to haunt someone. What could you possibly need my help with?"

"We need to find your father a new wife."

"Can we go back to my other idea? I think haunting would be so much easier." I sighed, suddenly overwhelmed with fatigue. "Dad is a hopeless case."

"You're tired. Sleep on it. They're sending you home tomorrow, and then we'll figure out what we're going to do."

It appeared I had no choice. I was going to be a ghost's accomplice in the matchmaking of my father.

Oh, this was going to be ghoulish all right.

No longer able to fight the exhaustion, I closed my eyes. And as I began the spiral down to unconsciousness, my grandmother the ghost hummed a soft lullaby until I drifted off to sleep.

CHAPTER 3

The next day, after the doctor came by and told me I was okay enough to leave, Dad came to the hospital and took me home.

I was still tired and pretty messed up over the whole I-can-hear-my-dead-grandmother thing, so we didn't talk much on the way. Dad did tell me that Mom and Stan caught a later flight and went on their honeymoon, so that was a relief. Although the way he said it, it was obvious he still wasn't over Mom having gotten remarried. I didn't have the energy to say anything about it, though.

"You should go get some rest," he said once we were inside the house.

I nodded. "I'd like something to eat." I looked into the fridge for something, anything, to tide me over.

"Unbelievable. I just can't believe this."

I turned to see Dad holding up the dress I'd been wearing at the wedding. I couldn't believe it either. It had several scorch marks and even a burn hole that went right through the fabric. If the electricity going through my body was enough to do that to the material, how did I survive?

The enormity of what had happened suddenly hit me, and I had to sit down. I shuffled over to the table and dropped into a chair, still staring at the dress. "I could have died."

Dad put down the dress and approached me. "But you didn't, and that's what matters."

I nodded, still feeling a bit overwhelmed.

"Come on, kid, let's go get you up to bed; you can have a snack later."

He took my hand and gently guided me out of the chair and up to my room.

"Do you need some help?" he asked as I kicked off my All Stars.

I'd sleep in my clothes before I'd let my dad help me get undressed, but I did appreciate that he offered. "No, I'm okay. Thanks."

He closed the gap between us and gave me a big hug. "I'm glad to see you're okay, kid." His voice hitched.

I fought my own tears; it was pretty messed up to think I had survived a lightning strike.

He left, closing the door behind him. I glanced over at my computer, dying to check my e-mail (my cell phone got toasted by the lightning, so I'd been totally incommunicado since). But my eyes, heavy and protesting any more use, would have no part of it. I gave in to the exhaustion, undressing and climbing in between the sheets.

My last thought before drifting off was that it seemed really quiet. Maybe my brain was a little fried from the lightning and I had dreamed up the whole thing.

That made a lot more sense than suddenly having the ability to hear dead people.

CHAPTER 4

My cat, Salvatore Lasagna, woke me up by kneading his paws all over my chest. I tried to push him away, but he certainly didn't care that I needed sleep after all the excitement of being hit by lightning. Cats are like that.

I looked at the clock: it was almost dinnertime.

My stomach growled its confirmation.

I got out of bed and put on a pair of yoga pants and a T-shirt before heading downstairs to raid the fridge. Halfway down the stairs I could smell pizza. Sometimes Dad knew just what I needed.

He wasn't in the kitchen, but the box was on the island so I flipped it open, grabbed two slices, put one on top of the other on a paper towel, and followed the TV sounds to the den. Dad was in there, reading his paper and scarfing down his own slices.

"Hi," I said, taking the spot next to him on the couch.

He lowered his paper and put the slice down on his plate. "Hey, kid, how're you feeling?"

I took a bite of my pizza and nodded. "Okay," I said, even though I wasn't supposed to talk and chew at the same time—I needed to get that pizza in my empty belly and fast. "What are you watching?"

He glanced over at the TV and winced even though it was on a commercial. "I guess it's *The Bachelor*. I wasn't really watching." He held his paper back up to make his point.

"Maybe he'll learn a few things," said someone who sounded distinctly like my dead grandmother. "He could use some tips on courting."

Oh, this is not good, I thought. *Courting?*

"Dad?" I asked.

"Mmmhmm?"

"What do you think happens when we die?"

He lowered the paper again. "What do you mean, Lilah?" His eyes softened and he cocked his head to the side. "You heard what the doctor said. You're going to be fine. Do you have a headache or anything?"

I shook my perfectly nonaching head. "No, I'm just wondering what happens after . . . you know."

"We come back to haunt our families. *Wooooooooo!*" my grandmother said.

Not funny.

Okay, it kind of was.

"Like where do you think Bubby is right now?" I asked, wondering if I should tell him. And if I did, would he even believe me? Probably not. He'd probably take me back to the hospital to have my head examined.

"I'm right beside you," she said. But of course, Dad didn't know that.

He took a deep breath. "I'm not really sure. Maybe she's in heaven playing mah-jongg with her friends. Or maybe she's down in Florida, watching over your grandfather."

"Not anymore. He's got that new girlfriend of his, Marilyn Feldman, to watch over him."

The way my grandmother said it, I could tell she was only joking about being jealous. She made it seem like after you die, you just want happiness for the people you left behind.

Maybe that's why she said, "Oy, Lilah, we need to find your father a new wife. Look at him; he has pizza sauce on his face."

I looked up and sure enough, Dad had sauce and even a string of cheese stuck on his cheek. I leaned over and wiped it away with my paper towel.

"I didn't know Zeyde has a new girlfriend," I said.

Dad leaned back and looked at me. "He doesn't. Wait . . . what?"

Oops, busted.

"Uh, I mean . . . Does Zeyde have a new girlfriend in Florida?"

Dad frowned and shook his head. "I don't think so, Lilah."

"Sure he does," Bubby said. "Marilyn wouldn't have been my first choice for him, but she's a good cook and he enjoys her company. Even though I'm a better bridge player. But it's nice to see him happy. Now, Lilah, don't go telling your father our little secret. He wouldn't get it, would he?"

I shook my head. She was right. He totally wouldn't get it. And he definitely wouldn't be on board with the whole finding him a wife thing.

"Good girl. Now don't fill up too much on that pizza!"

I was just thinking about how she hadn't changed, when she said, "Because your dad brought home a carton of Chunky Monkey!"

I took another bite of my pizza to hide my smile. Maybe hearing my dead grandmother was going to be pretty cool, after all.

After I ate, I returned to my room to call Alex and let her know I was okay.

She was very relieved to hear it and told me I had become an overnight celebrity at school. People couldn't wait to see me, the lightning-strike survivor.

I could tell she was disappointed when I told her I wouldn't be back to school until at least Wednesday.

I wanted to cheer her up, but wasn't sure I wanted to tell her about my grandmother yet. It was still kind of freaky. And what if it was just an aftereffect of the lightning? What if it was all in my head?

Keeping it a secret, at least for a little while, seemed like a good idea.

"Andrew Finkel asked me how you're doing, by the way."

My heart skipped in my chest. "What?"

"Yep," Alex said, sounding all smug. "He said he hopes you're okay."

"*How* did he say it?" It's imperative to know these details.

"How I just said it, '*I hope she's okay.*'"

"Do you think . . ." I couldn't even say it.

"Do I think what?"

"Nothing."

"What, Lilah?"

"Nothing. Really. Who else? Did the teachers say anything?"

"Well, in science class, Mrs. Campbell taught us

about lightning and the best ways to avoid being hit by it."

I snorted. "Too late!"

She laughed. "Well yeah, *for you*, but Anita was really freaked out, so at least everyone knows how it happened and how to be safe in storms."

I guess it was a good idea. Although I wished I could have been there. I was looking forward to my newfound notoriety. I'd never been famous for anything before.

And to think that Andrew Finkel asked about me . . .

"So, Lilah?" Alex asked quietly.

"Yeah?"

"Were you really scared?" I could tell by my best friend's voice that she was. I wonder what it must have been like for her to watch the ambulance take me away to the hospital. It was probably the scariest thing ever.

"I don't remember, to be truthful. I mean, one second I'm standing there and the next, I wake up in the hospital. I didn't even have a chance to *get* scared."

"I was scared," Alex said, and I could hear her crying. "I was scared you were dead."

"I'm sorry," I said.

"It's not your fault. But I'm glad the lightning didn't kill you. I'm really glad."

"So am I, Alex."

After a few minutes more, Alex had to go because her mom needed to use the phone, but she promised to call me right after school the next day to report on anything I missed.

After I hung up I took a deep breath, and it's like it all hit me at once. I began to cry really hard.

"Don't worry, Lilah," my grandmother said. "You're fine." And then I felt warm all over. Like I was getting a big hug from her.

Which is really weird, if you think about it.

CHAPTER 5

O h, kiddo, you don't have to do that," Dad said as he walked in the door from work and saw me cooking dinner. "You should be resting."

I didn't stop tearing the lettuce for the salad. "It's okay, I feel fine." Bored was more like it. I actually couldn't wait to get back to school.

He put his briefcase down and kicked off his shoes. "What are we having?"

"I defrosted some salmon for the barbecue. And I'm making salad and steamed asparagus."

"Good choice." Dad came into the kitchen and put his hand on my back. "You sure you're feeling up to this?"

I was about to say that if I could handle talking to my dead grandmother, I was up for tossing a salad, but I wasn't ready to tell Dad about my new ability. Not yet. Maybe never.

"Yeah, I'm okay," I said.

"You're a good girl, keeping me fed and happy," Dad said, picking a cherry tomato out of the salad and popping it into his mouth.

I thought about my grandmother's plea for help. Dad needed more than just his daughter in his life to make him happy. Bubby was so right. Dad totally needed to get out there and start meeting people. He wasn't the type to find anyone at work, since he was more of a head-down kinda guy (and I'd never even heard him mention any women at the insurance firm where he worked as an actuary).

And then there was that. He was an *actuary*. I wasn't sure what he did exactly, but it had to do with policies, numbers, and minimizing risk or something. Yawn.

"Hey, Dad?" I asked as he leaned over the sink to turn on the tap. One of his ways of "minimizing risk" was to wash his hands a thousand times a day. If he ever did find a woman, she was going to have to be a germophobe, too, or his hygiene habits would drive her nuts.

"Yes, honey?"

"Now that Mom's married . . ." His entire body stiffened at my words, but I powered through, determined to have this conversation. "Um, do you think that maybe you'll start dating?"

He seemed not to have heard me as he lathered up the soap and took great care to get the foam in between every finger and even under the wedding band he still wore.

"Where is this coming from, Lilah?" he finally asked after a good rinse. He was stalling; it was totally obvious.

"Well, I just thought it's been a long time, and you never go out or anything . . ."

Dad pushed the tap off with his elbow and looked at me, holding up his hands in front of him like he was a surgeon getting ready to remove an appendix. Then he reached for a paper towel ("Dish towels harbor germs, Lilah"). "I don't need to be dating."

That made no sense at all. "Dad."

He opened the fridge, rooting around for his nightly predinner glass of tomato juice.

"Dad!" I said again.

He turned back toward me, abandoning the juice. "What is it, Lilah?" It was like he had completely forgotten what I had said.

"You *do* need to be dating. I hate to be mean, but look at you, Dad. You're thirty-eight, single, and you spend every evening at home, drinking your tomato juice and either playing Scrabble with your daughter or watching TV by yourself. You're in a rut. You need to get out there before it's too late."

"I *like* playing Scrabble with my daughter." He almost sounded pouty. But it was a good thing; it meant he was actually listening.

I tilted my head and gave him that look. The one he gave me when *he* wasn't buying *my* story. "Really? You like it *that* much?"

He pulled out one of the kitchen chairs and sat down, a big sigh escaping him as he did. "Am I that pathetic, Lilah?"

I took the chair beside him. "I wouldn't say *pathetic*. Maybe just a little sad and in denial."

"Ouch."

"Sorry."

He shook his head. "Don't be. You're right." He reached out and grabbed my hand. "And thank you for caring enough to say so. I'm sure it's not easy to tell your old man he's *sad and in denial*."

"We worry about you, Dad."

He cocked his head. "Who's 'we'?"

Uh-oh. Where was my dead grandmother when I needed her? Here I was doing her dirty work and she was MIA.

"We," I said, making a big gesture with my arms. "*We*, like a *collective we*. You know." It was a total stretch, but there was a better chance that Dad would think I was a nut than guess his dead mother was the other part of who I meant when I'd said "we."

It seemed to satisfy him.

"I guess it's been long enough since the divorce."

"Yeah, she's not coming back, Dad."

"No kidding."

"Maybe you could go on an Internet dating site."

Dad groaned. "Doesn't that smack of desperation?"

I raised my eyebrows.

"Good point," he said. "I get it. How about this, though. George at work has been trying to fix me up with his divorced sister. I'll say yes to that, and if it doesn't go well, *then* I'll try the Internet thing."

I nodded. "That sounds fair."

We even shook on it. Mission accomplished.

It almost seemed *too* easy.

CHAPTER 6

The first day back at school started out like any other. Alex met me on the corner, and we continued on to the redbrick building that was our school.

I hadn't heard from my grandmother in over a day, so while Alex was droning on about how horrible our math test was (the one I'd missed the day before), I was beginning to think my powers had disappeared overnight.

Although it was a relief, I was a little sad. I hadn't had a chance to say good-bye to my grandmother and almost missed her presence.

But as I opened the door to school, countless voices hit me, like someone had turned on a thousand radios right in front of me. The force of it was overwhelming. I fell to my knees, dropping the door handle.

"Lilah?" Alex said, squatting down beside me.

I took a deep breath.

She shook my shoulder. "Lilah? You okay?"

Looking up at my friend, I nodded and took another breath. "I think there's something I need to tell you."

"You're not dying, are you?" Normally I would laugh at such a ridiculous question, but Alex's face was completely serious. It made sense that she was concerned, since she'd been really scared after I'd been hit by lightning.

I shook my head. "No, nothing like that. I . . ." I looked around to make sure we were alone. "Since the lightning, I have . . . I have abilities."

She frowned. "What?"

It felt bizarre to say it out loud, but there was no way Alex would ever guess. "I can hear spirits. Dead people."

"Shut up! You cannot."

"Yeah, I can."

She paused for a long time. "Like who?"

"My grandmother Dora."

Alex pulled me up so we were both standing. I winced at the pain in my knees. She crossed her arms and glared at me. "Your dead grandmother came back from the grave and is now talking to you?"

I nodded, knowing I sounded like a head case. "Honestly."

"And what kind of wisdom does good old Bubby Dora have from the great beyond?"

"She wants me to help Dad find a wife."

Alex fake gagged. "Ugh!"

"No kidding."

She leaned back and looked at me intently. "Are you seriously not making this up?"

I crossed my heart.

"Lilah Bloom, that is totally messed."

"Yeah, well, I thought maybe I'd dreamed it until just now."

"What do you mean?"

"When I opened the door. There's a ton of people just inside, trying to talk to me."

Alex pulled the door open a crack. The voices seeped out, so many of them talking at once that they were drowning out my consciousness.

"There's nobody there," Alex said, opening the door a bit wider. Pushing past her, I pressed it closed and shook my head.

"This is not going to work. There's too many."

"Too many what?"

"Voices. That's what I mean. My ability is back. And I think it's back with a vengeance."

She looked up at the school. "So there are dead people in there who want to talk to you?"

I shrugged. "I guess so."

"Freaky."

"Very."

"What are you going to do?"

"I have to go in."

"Are you sure?"

I nodded. "I have to, Alex, otherwise I'm going to flunk out."

Alex rolled her eyes. "Uh, are you kidding me? You're going to be a rich TV medium. You don't need no education."

"You're freaking hilarious. I'm going to tell them to back off."

"You think that will work?"

"I have no idea; let's give it a go."

Holding my breath, I grabbed the handle and opened the door. When the voices hit me I exhaled, straightened my spine, ignored how silly I felt, and said aloud, "I will *not* be speaking with any of you today. I am just returning to school and need some peace and quiet to catch up on my studies. I will address you when I'm good and ready!"

And just like that, the voices stopped.

Huh.

"'*Catch up on your studies*'?" Alex mocked me. "What is that all about?"

I shrugged and headed into the school.

First period (music), I was alone in one of the practice rooms, sitting at the drum kit with earphones on and my eyes closed, making an absolute massacre of my lesson. But as much as I was still kind of bad, I was definitely improving and was very pleased that I was able to follow the song better than I had even just the last time I practiced. It was coming more easily, like my hands were finally getting it.

I was about a third of the way into the song, drumming along with my eyes closed, when I felt a pressure on my arm. Startled, I threw my drumsticks in the air, narrowly missing my music teacher's head with one of them.

I pulled the earphones off my ears. "Oh no! Mr. Robertson, I'm so sorry!"

He reached over and hit the stop button on the CD player, cutting the music to the earphones. "You missed. And I'm the one who should be sorry. I didn't mean to startle you, Lilah. How's it going?"

"Getting better, I think."

"It sounds like it. You're making some good progress."

I shrugged. "Me and Alex want to start a band."

He nodded. "You two could really rock it out."

I really liked Mr. Robertson. He was maybe thirty or so. He wasn't all stiff and boring like some of the other teachers. You could imagine this guy was a kid once, not like Mr. Burrows, who lived and breathed math. You assumed that guy was *born* bald and middle-aged.

"You and Alex both have talent. You just need to practice, practice, practice."

I nodded. "I know. We're still not very good, but we're determined."

"Hey, Lilah, want to hear something really fun?"

"Yeah, for sure."

He grinned. "Okay, let me in there for a second."

I got up and retrieved my drumsticks from the floor, handing them to him.

"Thanks." Mr. Robertson took my spot on the stool, took a breath, and started drumming.

I was instantly awestruck.

The drumming was like nothing I'd ever heard before and certainly nothing I'd aspired to be able to do, at least not for many years. But Mr. Robertson was totally kicking it, his hands a blur as he hit the drums in all the right places. His face was lit up, like this was what he lived for, his passion.

I was in total awe.

When he finished, with a big cymbal crash, he turned to me. There was sweat on his forehead but he smiled. "So, what do you think?"

"That was awesome, Mr. Robertson. I didn't know you could play like that!"

"Practice, Lilah. You'll get there."

I seriously doubted it, but still, it was cool to watch my teacher drum like a rock star.

"What was that?"

He shrugged. "Just an old Van Halen song."

I'd never heard of Van Halen, but I was definitely going to look them up. Maybe my dad had one of their CDs.

"That was really so cool, Mr. Robertson," I said, taking the drumsticks from him. But as my hand touched the wood, a jolt of something went through me. I looked up into my teacher's face. "Ugh, did you feel that?"

He tilted his head as though he was listening for something. "Feel what?"

I looked down at the drumsticks. They seemed to be pulsing in my hands.

"The sticks, do they seem weird to you?"

He glanced down and shrugged. "They're not the kind I normally prefer to use, but there's nothing wrong with them."

"Oh, never mind," I said, feeling really stupid. I mentally willed my grandmother to come and explain what was going on.

No such luck.

Mr. Robertson let go of the sticks and got up off the stool.

"Bubby!" I coughed into my hand, hoping he didn't get that I was beckoning my dead grandmother to come help me decipher a new psychic quirk.

He turned around. "Bless you."

Clueless. Good. But apparently, so was my grandmother.

"So, are you in a band, Mr. Robertson?"

He shook his head. "I used to be, but most of the guys are married with jobs and kids now, so it's hard for us to get together and jam."

"That's sad. You're really talented. You shouldn't let that go to waste."

He smiled down at me. "It's not wasted. I get to watch kids like you develop your talent. Maybe someday your band will be famous and you'll give me free tickets, and I'll be able to tell everyone you were my student. That's good enough for me."

"Really? That's good enough?" I had my doubts. And when I asked, his smile receded a little. Just a little, but enough for me to see it.

"Ask him about jet-black wig," a woman's voice said from across the room.

There was no one there. How could there be? We were in a closed practice room.

A sick feeling landed in my stomach. I had told the spirits to go away today, but here was a cheeky one, determined to talk to me. "No," I said out loud, smoothing the hair down on my arms.

"Sorry, Lilah?"

I looked back at Mr. Robertson. "Sorry, I was just thinking of something."

He frowned. "Are you okay? You seem a little, I don't know, distant."

I shook my head. "No, I'm fine. I just thought I heard something."

He laughed. "Well, it's a soundproof room, so I can't see how."

"Ask him. Ask him about jet-black wig and you'll find out that teaching isn't enough for him."

The voice was like a finger, poking in my brain. Not letting go until I did as it demanded.

I took a deep breath. *Here we go again.* "Mr. Robertson, do you believe in ghosts?"

He blinked. "That's kind of an odd question to ask your music teacher, isn't it, Lilah?"

"Not as weird as you think. You know how I got hit by lightning last weekend?"

He nodded, still frowning. "Of course."

"Well, it seems that since then I have some sort of superpsychic powers."

He crossed his arms in front of his chest but didn't say anything.

"I hear voices."

"Lilah, do you want me to ask the nurse to call one of your parents to come get you?"

I shook my head. "No, I'm okay. Really, about the voices, I can prove it."

He arched his eyebrows, waiting.

"There is someone here in the room with us telling me to ask you about jet-black wigs, although I have no idea what that means."

Based on the way he dropped down onto the drum stool, *he* did.

"How could you know about that?"

"I'm telling you, there's someone here. A woman, telling me to ask you about jet-black wigs."

"Jet Black Wig was the name of the band I was in a decade ago. We were just about to sign a record deal when our lead singer died."

"That was me," the voice said.

"What was your lead singer's name?" I asked.

Mr. Robertson looked at me. "Her name was Serena."

"Yup, that's me."

"That's who's here. Serena."

"Lilah, you're fooling with me," Mr. Robertson said, suddenly not sounding so teacherlike. "You Googled me or something."

I shook my head. "Nope, I promise you I didn't. How did she die?"

"Cancer," Serena said.

"Car accident," Mr. Robertson said.

I looked at my teacher, wondering why he was lying. "She said it was cancer."

And then as I stood there, my music teacher began to cry. He covered his eyes with his hands and just lost it. "Serena, are you really here?"

"I'm here, Frankie," Serena said.

"She says yes." It felt kind of weird, watching him cry like that. I looked out the window into the main music room, but no one seemed to be paying any attention. Most of the kids were goofing off and talking instead of playing their instruments, but I wasn't about to point that out to Mr. Robertson. Grabbing a tissue from the pack in my bag, I handed it to him.

"Sorry to dump this on you," I said. "It seems spirits have figured out I can hear them, so they come to me, demanding to be heard."

He took the tissue and looked at me. "I'm sorry. You shouldn't be seeing me like this. It's just a bit overwhelming."

"It's okay," I said. "It's pretty overwhelming for me, too."

"Tell him he's a jerk for not keeping the band together."

I relayed the message.

"Can she hear me?" he asked me.

I nodded.

"Serena, there was no moving on after you . . . were gone. I couldn't. I just couldn't."

I was beginning to think they were more than just bandmates, but kept my mouth shut.

"Tell him to get the band back together."

"She wants you to get the band back together."

"Oh, Serena, I can't do that."

"Tell him he has to. Tell him that Phil Rivers is working at Sony now and he'll remember us."

I relayed the message.

"Phil Rivers," Mr. Robertson said.

I shrugged.

"He was the guy at the label that was going to sign us. But Serena, he was just at an indie label. If he's at Sony now, he'll never want to sign a garage band like us."

Serena seemed to not want to take no for an answer. "Frankie, you have to. Period."

I told him what she'd said. I also told him if he didn't, Serena promised to haunt me until he complied.

"Nice tactic," Serena said. "You're a sassy one, aren't you?"

"Fine then," Mr. Robertson said finally. "I guess I've been thinking about it lately, anyway, how it would be cool to try again. Okay, fine. I'll call the guys and see about getting the band back together."

"Good. Mission accomplished," Serena said, her voice softer now.

Then she surprised me by talking *to* me and not just *through* me. "Lilah, If you'd heard the band, you'd understand how important it is that they get back together. We were going places. They *will* go places, even with another singer. Thank you for your help. I've been waiting a decade for this opportunity."

"You're welcome."

"And I'm sorry if this is kind of weird for you," she continued. "But can you please tell him I love him?"

It *was* weird, but how could I not? So I did, which just made Mr. Robertson cry more (which just made it weirder for me, of course).

"I love you, too, Serena, and still miss you so much."

Serena was quiet for a long time. But just as I was about to ask her if she was still there, she spoke up. "Enough for now. Lilah, tell him I'm leaving. And that I look forward to seeing him onstage with the guys."

I told him what she'd said and that she was gone.

Mr. Robertson wiped at his eyes with the now tattered tissue. After several weird minutes, he finally spoke. "Are you okay with all this, Lilah? This sudden gift you have seems like a real double-edged sword."

I thought about how I'd silenced the spirits at the door that morning and straightened my spine, determined. "Yeah, I'll be okay. Just don't go advertising this around. I don't need Ms. Francutti breathing down my neck thinking I'm a psycho." I had little reason to think Mr. Robertson would rat me out to the school social worker, but still, you gotta make sure.

He nodded and put his hand on my arm. "I won't say anything to anyone. And Lilah, thank you. I can't say thank you enough."

"You're welcome. I'll just take some free passes to *your* show as payment, okay?"

He grinned. "Deal. Now I'd better get back out there and do some actual teaching."

The bell rang, signaling the end of class.

We both laughed. I grabbed my bag while he stood up and reached for the door. My stomach growled. Seems this psychic work makes one very hungry.

So as if I wasn't frazzled enough after that, I was walking down the hall toward my math class when I saw Andrew Finkel. Wow, he was so cute. His hair was all shaggy like he just got out of bed, but it really suited him. And those eyes . . .

Suddenly, he looked right at me and opened his mouth to say something.

Ah!

I freaked out a little and hurried past him, ducking into the bathroom. I had no reason *not* to talk to him, other than I'd surely sound like an idiot, all stuttering and nervous. Best not to put myself in that situation.

Needing to kill a minute or two until he was gone from the hall, I checked myself out in the mirror. Hair was good, now teeth.

"You look fine."

I looked around to find the source of the voice. But there wasn't anyone there. There was one girl peeing in the stall, but I knew it wasn't her who'd spoken. And, anyway, the voice sounded like a grown woman.

"Pardon?" I said quietly.

"I said, you look good. You don't have anything stuck in your teeth."

"Thanks," I said, dryly, running the water so I wouldn't be heard talking to myself.

"But your outfit is a disaster."

"What?" I looked down. I was wearing my comfy cargo capris and flip-flops with my favorite T-shirt.

"The baggy look is out. And flip-flops? Please."

"I didn't ask for your opinion," I said. "I don't even know who you are."

The girl in the stall came out and joined me at the sinks to wash her hands.

It was Dolly Madison. Her real name was Dorothy, but she liked to be called Dolly, which Alex thought was stupid, because who would want to be named after a snack-cake company, anyway. I didn't bother telling Alex about Dolley Madison, the First Lady from a long time ago who was so famous, she'd even made it onto a coin.

Someday, Alex would figure that one out on her own.

Anyway, Dolly was in eighth grade and was popular with the boys because she was tall and had boobs, something she and I certainly didn't have in common. Her boobs and the subsequent attention from members of the opposite sex made her kind of snobby and mean to other girls. Especially younger girls without boobs.

Girls like me.

She looked me up and down before saying very sarcastically, "Nice pants."

"See? I told you so," said the disembodied fashion critic.

I straightened my shoulders. "I like these pants."

Dolly rolled her eyes so far, they almost disappeared. "Whatever. Although they do take the focus off your chest."

See what I mean? Harsh. It would have made me sad, but I knew my boobs were coming. No one stays flat forever.

Right?

With a loud snort, Dolly turned to leave the bathroom. But before she got to the door, she tripped and fell flat on her face!

I couldn't help it—I laughed.

"You tripped me!" she yelled as she got up.

I did a double take. Was she really accusing me of tripping her? "Did not!"

She stared at me as she rubbed her elbow, cringing like it really hurt. "I know you tripped me. I didn't just fall."

I tried not to cry, even though I knew I hadn't done it. "I'm way over here, I couldn't have tripped you even if I wanted to!" And I really kind of wanted to. She was SO mean!

She opened her mouth to say something else, but instead just huffed, turned away, and finally left the bathroom.

"What a horrible girl!" the voice from before said.

"Who are you?" I asked.

"Priscilla Lafontaine."

"Who?"

"Oh! Lilah," my grandmother showed up out of the blue. "Ms. Lafontaine is the epitome of fashion! She was a wonderful designer and you should consider it an honor that she gave you fashion advice. I just loved your fashions, Ms. Lafontaine!"

"Oh, thank you, Dora, I so miss working in fashion since I crossed over. But please, call me Prissy."

Oh, maybe that *explains it*, I thought while the dead old women struck up a conversation like they were having high tea or something. Maybe this Prissy person used to make old lady clothes.

I looked back down at my capris. I liked them. I liked them a lot. And really, that's all that matters, right? I mean, isn't it?

Although I was beginning to feel a bit self-conscious.

Great. My self-esteem was getting a beating from ghosts.

Like being twelve and having no boobs wasn't bad enough.

"Don't do it."

"Don't do wha . . . ?" I turned to say, but there was no one there.

I returned to what I was doing, which was ordering lunch in the cafeteria.

"I'll have the meat loaf, please."

"Ugh. I said don't!"

As I waited for the lunch lady to dish out my portion, I discreetly looked around.

"I told you all to leave me alone today," I said, trying to keep my lips from moving.

"This is important. Do you really want to eat something disgusting? I'm doing you a favor!"

I took the plate of food and put it down on my tray.

"Who are you?"

"Someone who knows disgusting meat loaf when she sees it."

I looked down at the square of bumpy meat, which had been smothered in gray sludge.

"Stick with the salad, honey," the ghost said.

Maybe it wasn't a bad idea, after all. I slid the tray to the end of the line and then abandoned it there, grabbing a salad from the fridge instead.

"Good choice; you won't regret it."

I turned toward the big milk dispenser and pulled the lever on the spout while I asked, "Who are you really?"

"My name's Marion, and I was the lunch lady here at this school for forty-nine years before I passed four years ago."

"Wow, that's some job commitment," I said.

"Oh, honey, I just loved working here so much, I couldn't bear to leave! Not retirement or even death could keep me from coming and seeing you kids every day."

I was thinking maybe Miss Marion needed a life, but uh . . . well, I guess she didn't have a choice anymore.

"Well, thanks for the warning."

"You're welcome, honey, the new cook ain't what old Phil was before he retired."

I took my salad and my milk to the counter and handed the cashier my lunch card.

"Have a wonderful day, honey!" the dead lunch lady said.

"You, too," I said back, scanning the crowd for Alex.

She was not gonna believe this.

The rest of the afternoon was quiet, spirit-wise, so by the end of fourth period, I'd almost forgotten about my new powers.

And it had turned into a very long day.

I ended up eating my lunch by myself, forgetting that Alex had badminton club at lunch on Wednesdays.

So that was horrible; if I'd remembered I was

going to be on my own, I would have just grabbed a sandwich and then eaten by my locker instead of sitting in the cafeteria waiting for my best friend who was never going to come.

And I definitely wouldn't have sat there if I'd known that I would be subjected to question after question about being hit by lightning from like every kid in school.

It seemed I was quite the novelty.

The most popular question was, "Did you buy a lottery ticket?" since I seemed to be so very lucky to have survived a lightning strike. After the seventh time I was asked, I stopped answering with, "Uh, hello, you have to be eighteen to buy lottery tickets," and started answering with, "Yes, as a matter of fact, I did, and no, I will not be sharing my millions with you, moron." Okay, well, I kept the moron part to myself, but really. *Duh.*

So when Alex caught up with me at my locker and asked if I'd heard any other voices, I stared at her for a superlong time before I realized what she meant.

"Oh, sorry, I'm so tired I actually forgot." I reached into my locker for my math book and shoved it into my backpack.

"How could you possibly forget that you hear—"

I slammed my locker door closed, stopping her from finishing her sentence.

"*Shhh.* Not here, Alex."

Her mouth formed an O as she finally picked up on my apprehension. But knowing Alex, she could erupt with an inappropriate comment at any time.

Grabbing her arm, I led her out of the school before anyone heard her talking about my new ability.

"Ow, Lilah, let go," Alex whined as we got to the door.

"Sorry," I said, dropping her arm. "I just needed to get out of there."

"Everything okay?"

I looked around to make sure no one was within earshot. "Yeah, I'm just really tired."

"Yeah?" Alex was looking at me intently, waiting for me to spill.

"Okay. The biggest thing was an incident in music class."

Her eyes went wide. "The *biggest* thing? What happened?"

"So I was practicing in the drum room, and Mr. Robertson comes in, and his dead bandmate shows up and tells me I have to make him get his old band back together."

"No kidding!"

I nodded. "For real."

"So what did you do?"

"I told him she wanted them to get the band back together."

"Wow," Alex said.

Sometimes Alex could be a little thick.

"It's so cool that you are psychic now. And now we know it's not just people you know who speak to you." Her face suddenly got serious. "Hey, do you think . . ."

"Do I think what?"

"You could probably even get *paid* for it."

I looked at her sideways. "What do you mean?"

"Oh, come on, you've seen psychics on TV. I know you have. Remember that one who solved crimes and told some lady in the audience to get her thyroid checked?"

I didn't like where this was going. "Yeah, I remember."

"You can get *paid* for being a medium and giving people messages from their dead friends and family. People will pay tons of money for that stuff." She grabbed my arm. "Lilah, just think about it! We could make so much money! We could get you your drum set and me a guitar, and we can really start our band!"

I still didn't think it was a good idea, hiring myself out as a medium, especially since I had no idea if I even *could* talk to dead people at will. So far they had come to me. But Alex was so excited, and the prospect of finally getting my own drum set was kind of awesome.

And then there was the whole helping people bit. Since I was really little, I always thought I'd want to be a nurse or a social worker because the thought of helping people really appealed to me.

Of course, "medium" is not an option they explore on Career Day, but after what happened with Mr. Robertson and even getting dad to start dating, I was beginning to think maybe I'd found my calling. It felt really good to relay messages and give people peace and closure they wouldn't get any other way. That part of it was totally cool.

Alex stared at me, waiting for my answer, hoping I was in on her new plan.

I took a deep breath. "Okay, let's do it."

The next day a whole bunch of kids and even a couple of teachers were absent from school. No one knew why, but when I got home from school and was making dinner, Dad put on the news and we heard a story about a terrible case of food poisoning at our school.

Apparently it was the meat loaf.

"Thank you, lunch lady," I said.

CHAPTER 7

Dad was nervous, and of course I wasn't helping, but there was no way I could let him go on a date wearing what he had on. I was just thankful he'd stopped at the barber on his way home to fix his uncooperative hair, or we'd have had to do a total makeover on him.

"What's wrong with this?" he asked, holding out his arms to give me the full view. As if I needed to see the whole package to know he was a fashion *DON'T*.

"Oy," my grandmother said, her first word in days. Even though she scared me half out of my skin, I felt suddenly warm knowing she was there.

"There is so much wrong with this, Dad. I don't even know where to start."

He swallowed, looking like maybe he was going to throw up.

Clearly, I needed to be gentler. He was obviously very fragile. "Sorry, I didn't mean to be heartless. Let's start with where you're going."

"Dinner."

"Where?"

"Frangelico's."

"A steak house?"

He nodded.

"Her choice or yours?"

"Mine. I thought the man was supposed to decide."

"Sure. In 1950," Bubbly said.

I bit back the sigh; no use making it worse. "Did you at least ask her if it was okay?"

Dad was looking positively green. "No."

"I hope she's not one of those vegetarians," Bubby said, echoing my own thoughts. But I wasn't going to say it out loud to make him even more nervous. I mean, you would hope that if Dad's date was, in fact, a vegetarian, she would have told him. How cruel would it be to tell a man you'll go out to dinner with him just to have him take you to a steak house if you're a vegetarian?

"What should I have done?" Dad asked, so clueless it was almost cute.

Almost.

"Never mind that now. We need to fix what you're wearing."

"Oy, thank goodness, Lilah," my grandmother said. "At least you have sense enough not to let him go out *like that*."

I wanted to talk to her, but the current crisis would not allow for a tête-à-tête with a ghost. And, anyway, there would be plenty of time to chat once Dad left for his date.

I reached up and undid his tie while he stood there like an anxious, sweating mannequin, suffering through being dressed. "First, we need to get rid of this." I pulled off the tie and unbuttoned the first two buttons of his shirt, leaving a little neck showing but no chest hair.

"Not too casual?" Dad asked.

"No, it's perfect because you're still wearing the jacket. But, um . . ." I cocked my head, mentally going through Dad's wardrobe, trying to pick a more suitable sport coat.

"The camel one would look better," Bubby said.

"Yeah, you're right." I nodded.

"Who's right?" Dad said, looking down at me.

Whoops!

"Oh, sorry, Dad. I was just thinking your camel jacket would look better than this one. I guess I was just thinking out loud."

"The camel one, huh?"

Whew!

"Yeah."

Dad disappeared up the stairs to change his jacket, giving me a moment alone with my grandmother.

"I'm glad you're back, Bubby."

"I never totally left."

"How come I couldn't hear you?"

She sighed. "As much as I love being around you, I have things to do elsewhere. I can't be around all the time. I've noticed you're not sleeping so well, though."

Okay, my dead grandmother was watching me sleep (or more accurately, not sleep)? That's just creepy.

"I guess all of this is a lot to take in."

"I understand. I heard about your music teacher."

I nodded. "Yeah. I guess I'm learning all about what it means to . . . well, I don't know. Do what I do."

"Just be careful, Lilah. You can't be all things to all people."

"So what do you mean you have things you have to do elsewhere?" I asked, suddenly quite curious about how my grandmother spent her days.

"I have obligations."

"You're not going to tell me, are you?"

"Nope." I could even hear the smile in her voice. "Now be quiet, Lilah. Your father is coming down the stairs."

I turned and sure enough, there was Dad, looking great in his camel jacket. Good thing he had us as his stylists.

"So?"

I nodded approvingly. "Definitely much better."

He exhaled.

"You'll do great, Dad. Remember, Alex and I will be here watching a movie, so just duck into the bathroom and call if you need any tips or pointers."

"I hardly think I need help from my twelve-year-old daughter on how to date."

But his face said otherwise.

"Ya, right. Whatever you say."

He grabbed his car keys off the table by the front door and took one last look in the mirror on the back of the closet door.

"You look great. Now get going." I gave him a gentle push toward the front door, ignoring the pounding in my own chest. It was hard not to catch his nervousness. This was a monumental event.

He leaned down to give me a kiss on the cheek. "See you later. I shouldn't be too late."

"Lilah," my grandmother hollered. "The ring!"

"Dad!" I grabbed his arm.

"What?"

I held up his hand. "Take off your wedding band!"

He blushed as he slid the ring off his finger and handed it to me. "What would I do without you?"

I rolled my eyes and shoved him out the door.

"So," I said to my grandmother. "You think it'll go okay?"

Silence.

"Bubby?"

Still nothing.

And that's when it occurred to me. *She went with him!*

Not that I blamed her. I would have done the same. And at least she could report back on the disaster it was sure to be. But she could have at least said something before she left.

Just as I turned to go plant myself on the couch to wait for Alex, there was a knock at the door.

"Hey, Li. Your dad looked really good tonight," she said as she pushed past me, her bloated backpack whacking me in the shoulder.

I let out an *oof* and closed the door behind her. "What do you have in your bag?"

She headed right into the den and sat on the couch, bending down to open her backpack. I followed, repeating my question.

Alex looked up at me as though her bag was see-through and I could see for myself what was inside. "Uh, duh, Lilah." She held up a stack of multicolored pages. "Flyers, of course."

"Oh yes," I said. "Of course. Flyers." I sat down next to her. "Uh, flyers for what, exactly?"

"Oh, Lilah, you can be so clueless sometimes." She shook her head. "For our new business."

Oh. Right.

"You did up flyers?" I grabbed the top page, a lime-green sheet, off the pile.

Do you miss a loved one?
Want to know your future?
Wish you could talk to the dead?
Now you can . . .

JUST $5
FOR A FIFTEEN-MINUTE READING!

Located in the library
— media room 6 —
daily at lunch.

"So?" Alex asked, giddy and almost to the point where she was clapping her hands in excitement.

I returned the sheet to the top of the pile. "I

don't know. I can't tell people's future. How can I say that?"

Alex waved me off. "It doesn't matter. People won't care. When they hear their dead Grammy telling them to eat their peas, they'll be so shocked, they'll forget the rest."

"We could always haunt people," a boy's voice said. I looked around, knowing even as I did that no one else was in the room.

"Haunt people?" I asked.

Alex blinked. "Can you do that?"

I shook my head. "No, there's someone here who's talking about haunting people. But no, I'm totally not into that."

"Are you sure?" the boy said. "It could be fun!"

"No," I said firmly. "Please go away. I'm not going to do that."

"Humph," the boy said. But after a few minutes, he didn't say anything else, so I figured he was gone.

"So," I said to Alex. "When am I supposed to eat lunch if I'm spending all of my lunch periods doing readings for people?"

She stared at me like *I* was the one being ridiculous.

"I just don't know, Alex. I'm really not comfortable with this. You know, the flyers and everything. I was thinking if we were going to do this, it would be a little more low-key."

"I thought you wanted to help people?"

"I do," I said. "But it's just . . . this is a lot to take in. Maybe later, once I'm more used to it, you know?"

Alex seemed to get it. "Okay, I'm sorry. I didn't mean to push you. I was just hoping to start making some money so we could start our band."

"Well, have our babysitting certificates, why don't you make up some flyers for *that*, and we can put those around the neighborhood?"

Alex scrunched up her face. "Babysitting is not glamorous. Being a *medium* is glamorous."

"No, babysitting isn't glamorous, you're right. But it will get us instruments. Means to an end, Alex."

"Fine. Okay. I'll make up some babysitting flyers."

"So, what movies did you get?" I craned my neck, looking in her bag to see what DVDs she had brought over.

"Look! I got this out of the bargain bin at Walmart."

"Bargain-bin movies, Alex?"

She smiled and handed me the case. "Don't be a movie snob."

I groaned. "*Ghostbusters*?"

She shrugged, obviously quite pleased with herself. "Consider it educational."

"Whatever. You put it in and I'll go make popcorn."

Not much later—*Ghostbusters* was still on and you know what? It was pretty good!—Dad was back.

"We're in here," I hollered. Alex and I exchanged glances as we waited for Dad to take off his shoes and join us in the den. "It's too early; this can't be good," I said quietly to Alex while I stroked Salvatore Lasagna's soft fur.

"It's not," Bubby said.

"Oh no, what did he do?"

My grandmother sighed. "Let's just say we have a lot of work to do."

I looked at Alex and shook my head. "Apparently it didn't go well, but don't let on."

Alex zipped her lips and pasted a smile on her face just as Dad appeared in the doorway, still looking good, except for the huge grease stain down his front.

And the hunched shoulders.

Oh, and the frown of the defeated.

"Oh no! What happened?"

Dad didn't say anything as he stepped into the room and sat on the big recliner.

"Mr. Bloom, is everything okay?"

Dad gave Alex a half smile. A very unconvincing half smile. "Well, I didn't kill her, if that's what you're asking."

"Oy." I cringed, afraid to even hear what happened.

"Did you like her? Was she pretty?" Alex asked, obviously not getting that none of these things mattered, since it was clear Dad wouldn't be going out with George's sister again, no matter how pretty she was.

Dad looked at Alex, as incredulous as I. "She was a nice lady."

"So what happened, Dad?" Maybe we should just get this out so he could move on. Date one was just for practice, anyway. "She wasn't a vegetarian, was she?" I could almost see Dad ordering a big T-bone and his tree-hugging vegan date picking it up and throwing it at him in protest.

He shook his head. "No, it wasn't that. We were at the bar, waiting for our table, and she dropped her keys. When she bent down to get them, she tripped a waiter and guess who got a plate of fried calamari down the front of him?"

"Yum, calamari," Alex mused, quite inappropriately.

"Oh, Dad, that's awful." I shook my head, sympathetic to his first-date bad luck. "Did you at least like her?" I asked.

He shrugged. "I thought she was nice, but I'm sure I blew it."

"He did," Bubby said with a huge sigh. "He talked about earthquakes and asteroids."

"You didn't talk about natural disasters and probabilities and stuff, did you?"

He nodded, obviously realizing he'd made a mistake. "I couldn't help it. I was nervous."

Even Alex cringed.

"That's it. No more Discovery Channel for you."

"I forgot how hard dating is."

I shook my head. "No, you didn't. *Knowing* how hard dating is, is precisely what kept you from doing it all this time."

He looked at me and nodded. "You're probably right."

"I'm proud of you, though, Dad. You got out there and that's the hardest part. The next one will be easier."

"Next one?" he asked, looking a bit green. "There's going to be a next one?"

"Yes, next one. We're not giving up on you just yet."

"That's my girl," Bubby said. "We'll find him

another girl to go out with. I think my old bridge partner, Marjorie, has a daughter who's divorced since I died."

Is it wrong that I totally pitied Marjorie's daughter?

CHAPTER 8

Tamsin McNeil's birthday party was on Sunday. And it was a sleepover, my absolute favorite kind of birthday party! It was Memorial Day weekend, which meant no school on Monday, so it worked out perfectly.

The extravaganza was to begin with dinner on Sunday night, so Dad drove me to Tamsin's house (stopping to pick up Alex on the way) at five.

"What are you going to do tonight, Dad?" I asked, a little concerned.

"Oh, I don't know, soak my favorite shirt in Oxi-Clean?"

"That's sad," I said.

He looked at me. "I was just kidding. Since my mad dad skills are not required tonight, Fred and I are going out to a movie."

Mad dad skills? Oy.

I didn't comment. Thankfully, by that time, we were in front of Tamsin's house.

"I'll call tomorrow when we need a pickup, okay?"

He nodded. I leaned over and gave him a kiss on the cheek. "Have a nice time at the movie."

"See you, Mr. Bloom," Alex said as she got out of the backseat.

"Have fun, girls."

We walked up to the house together, each of us with our gifts, sleeping bags, pillows, and overnight bags in tow. "What does she have planned?" I asked Alex.

She shrugged. "She said something supersecret but guaranteed to be awesome."

"Everyone says that."

Tamsin was turning thirteen (on Tuesday, actually, but you can't have a party on a Tuesday), which for us normally meant a bar or bat mitzvah and not a regular party, but Tamsin isn't Jewish, so she got a regular party. My birthday is in December and Alex's is in November, but our parents all decided spring bat mitzvahs are much nicer than winter ones, so ours are both next June. I hope I still get to have some sort of celebration so my turning thirteen doesn't go unnoticed until MANY months later. But of course, I'm sure Dad will let me do *something*.

Alex pushed the doorbell and we waited for Tamsin to come to the door and let us in. It wasn't Tamsin who opened the door, but her older brother Mark.

Alex blushed the second she saw him. "Hi, Mark," she said.

Mark was in ninth grade, so in a whole different school from us. We hadn't seen him in a long time. Well, let me tell you, time had been good to him. He was way taller than I remembered, and his hair was all long and shaggy around his face. *Très* cute! He had a few zits, but they weren't horrible. He still looked good.

"They're in the basement," he said, not bothering to even say hi as he closed the door behind us.

"How's ninth grade?" Alex asked. She actually had googly eyes.

"S'okay," Mark said.

I grabbed my friend's arm and dragged her toward the stairs. "Come *on*, Alex."

She resisted, but then Mark turned and headed down the hall toward the kitchen, so she had no choice but to come with me.

"He got hot!" she whispered.

"You say that about every guy."

"I mean it. Why didn't Tamsin tell us her brother got so cute?"

"Maybe because she didn't want you ogling him!"

We were the last to arrive. Fiona Stevens, Sherise Thompson, and Anita Yee were already downstairs with Tamsin, sitting on the couches and watching *America's Next Top Model.*

"Hey!" I said.

Tamsin jumped up and ran over to hug us both. "Thanks for coming!"

I handed over her gift. "Happy almost birthday!"

"Thanks! I hope it's what I think it is!"

I hoped she thought it was a gift certificate for the Gap, because that's what it was. With the wedding and the lightning strike and all, I didn't really have time to get Dad to take me to the mall to get her something well thought out. Instead, he picked up the gift card on his way home from work on Thursday.

Alex handed her the gift she brought, which was a makeup kit we'd all seen at the mall a few weeks back and had agreed was awesome because it had everything all together in one place AND was coordinated for your colors by season. Tamsin looked best in cool colors, so her kit was called Winter. Mine, which I was hoping to get once I saved up enough money, was Autumn.

"Thanks, Alex," Tamsin said, placing the gifts on a side table with the rest. "We're going to watch *ANTM*, and then my mom will order the pizza. I have something really special for later."

She was grinning, so I could tell she was really excited about whatever it was that she had planned for us.

Alex and I took spots together on the floor and joined in critiquing the models' performances. We loved this show. We all had (not so) secret dreams of being on it one day, although we promised we wouldn't be all catty and mean to each other. Sometimes we had little disagreements, but mostly we did all get along.

At least we *did*. Until that very night.

CHAPTER 9

After the pizza, we returned to the basement, all excited for what was to come. Tamsin disappeared into the smelly storage room and then emerged a few seconds later with a box. It looked like a board game and my heart sank. I didn't want to play Monopoly or something lame like that.

But Tamsin had that twinkle in her eye.

"What is it?" Sherise asked.

Tamsin sat down and put the ratty old box down on the floor between us. "It's a Ouija board."

"What's a Ouija board?" Anita asked.

Tamsin took the lid off. "It's a special communication board. You ask spirits to come and talk to you."

Alex nudged me with her foot. I glared at her to keep her quiet.

"Oh, I don't like the sound of that," Anita said, sounding scared.

"Don't be frightened," Tamsin said. "We get to ask it questions."

"Who answers?" Fiona asked.

"See this?" Tamsin held up a teardrop-shaped piece of plastic with legs. "We all put our hands on this, and then the spirits guide us to the answer on the board." She pulled the board out of the box and laid it on the floor. It had all the letters of the alphabet on it, and also a YES in the top-left corner and a NO in the top-right corner. At the bottom it had GOOD BYE. There were also some mystical sun and moon drawings on it.

"I don't like this at all," Anita said.

Tamsin glared at her. "Then you don't have to play."

"Where did you get this?" Fiona asked.

"I got it at a garage sale, but the lady I bought it from said it had been in her family for generations, and that it was very lucky."

"If it was so lucky," Alex said, "why was she selling it at a garage sale?"

Tamsin shrugged. "I guess it had already brought them all the luck they needed. Are we going to do this or what?"

"You're all going to get possessed by ghosts,"

Anita said, moving back away from the board. "Maybe she was selling it because it's haunted."

I looked closely at the board, wondering if it was legit. "Hey," I said. "It says Parker Brothers on it. I bet you can buy this at Walmart."

"Still . . ." Anita was obviously freaked out.

"I think it's all hooey," I said, but quietly under my breath.

"It is," my grandmother answered, giving me a little shiver.

"Oh. Okay. Good to know." I leaned toward Alex. "Bubby says it's all a crock."

She nodded. "I thought so." She winked at me, though. She had that look in her eye that told me she was up to no good.

"Okay, girls," she said loudly so everyone would pay attention. "Let's get this started." She moved closer to the board and nodded at the rest of us to do the same.

We shuffled in. Well, all but Anita.

"Tamsin, it's your birthday party, so you should get to go first. Do you have a question ready?"

"Yes," she said, bouncing a little in her seat.

"Okay," Alex said, obviously taking over. "Everyone put your fingertips on the thingie."

We all did. Of course, except Anita, who was watching from her spot in the corner.

"Okay, Tamsin. What's your question?"

Tamsin took a breath. "Who will I marry?"

Everyone gasped. We all knew Tamsin was currently crushing on Tyler Landis, an eighth grader. He was an excellent hockey player who hoped to one day make it to the NHL. Alex liked to tease Tamsin that her future boyfriend wouldn't have any teeth, but Tamsin said with his NHL contract, he'd be able to buy himself a whole mouth full of teeth.

Personally, I'd rather my husband have his own natural teeth, thank you very much. But I guess Tamsin wasn't bothered by dentures.

All of a sudden, the plastic thing started to skitter and move under our fingers.

"Oh!" Anita yelped.

It was moving over toward the left side of the board.

"Where's the *T*?" Tamsin said. "Oh. Never mind."

Suddenly the piece started moving back toward the center. Toward the *T*.

I glanced at Alex, who looked at me and we both knew: it wasn't being guided by any spirits. It was totally being guided by Tamsin.

"She won't be marrying him," my grandmother said. "He likes Emily Hadley."

I nodded. Figures he'd like an eighth grader.

Alex nudged me. "What?"

"Tyler likes Emily Hadley," I whispered.

"No kidding?" Alex whispered back.

I nodded.

"Well, she does have boobs," Alex said.

"Oh, it's spelling out T-Y-L-E-R!" Tamsin squealed.

Fiona, Sherise, and even Anita squealed along with her.

"Okay, my turn," Alex proclaimed. I wondered why she would bother, since she knew it wasn't real.

"Who will I marry?"

Under my fingertips, I could feel the thing moving towards the *M*. *M* as in "Mark." Surprise, surprise.

"Stop pulling it, Alex!" Fiona said with a cluck of her tongue.

"I'm not! It wants to move to the *M*."

"*M*?" Tamsin said. "Who's an *M*?"

"Your brother."

Tamsin frowned. "No, you can't marry my brother."

"Why not?"

"Because you can't, that's all."

Alex got mad. "You think I'm not good enough for your precious brother?"

"That's not it. He's older than you."

"Only by two years. So who cares?"

I looked at Sherise, who shrugged.

Then I looked at Anita, whose eyes were so full of tears, they were going to spill over any second.

"Anita?" I said, bringing all the attention to her.

She looked down, causing two big tears to fall out of her eyes onto the carpet.

"Tamsin," I said, turning to her. "What's going on?"

"Nothing."

"Come on, what's wrong?"

She sighed. "This is my birthday party and I want to have fun, okay?"

"Fun? Did someone say fun?" a man said.

I looked around, but there were no men in the room.

"Who's there?" I said, before I realized the words were even out of my mouth.

The girls looked at me and then toward the stairs.

"Mark?" Tamsin hollered. "Go back upstairs!"

But it wasn't him. There was a spirit in the room—one only I could hear.

"You okay?" Alex asked quietly.

"Someone's here."

"What's with all the whispering?" Tamsin asked. "No whispering."

"Why are you crying, Anita?" Sherise asked, shuffling over to console Anita.

"Never mind," she said, wiping her tears away. Everyone focusing on her allowed me to find out who was with us. I got up and went into the little bathroom, turning on the light before I closed the door.

"Who's there?" I whispered.

"Chuckles."

"Chuckles?" What a weird name.

"Chuckles the clown."

You've got to be kidding, I thought. "What are you doing here?"

"This is a birthday party, isn't it?"

Involuntarily, I sighed. "Yes, but we're not toddlers. Don't you think we're a little old for a clown?"

"You're never too old for a clown!" He sounded very sure of it.

I certainly wasn't.

"Can't you go find some six-year-old's party to crash?"

He sounded sad when he said, "It's not the same if people can't hear me and know I'm just trying to have fun with them. I'm not mean; I'm not trying to scare anyone."

"What do you mean?"

"Think about being at a party, and all of a sudden balloons start blowing themselves up and twisting into animals. Do you think you would like that or would you be terrified?"

I thought it would be cool, but saw his point. I guess if I didn't know what was going on, that would be pretty scary.

But I had an idea. "Can you really do that? Make balloon animals?"

"Yes, and I can do magic tricks, although I guess you wouldn't be able to see them."

"Do you have balloons?"

All of a sudden, about twenty long, skinny balloons appeared in front of me. "Okay, cool. Give me some time to break the news to the girls, and then you can put on your show. How's that?"

"Really?" Chuckles sounded so happy.

"Sure, why not. It's better than that lame Ouija board."

"Oh, thank you, Lilah. Thank you!"

"You're welcome. When was the last time you did a real party? Like . . . when you were alive?"

"Oh, it's been ages. It was . . . let me think . . . 1964."

Wow, that was way before my dad was even born.

I left the bathroom after flushing the toilet and running the tap for a second so no one would wonder what I was doing in there.

But they probably wouldn't have noticed, anyway, because when I came out of the bathroom, I walked right into the middle of a fight.

"Why is *she* good enough and I'm not?" Alex said, right in Tamsin's face.

"I never said that." Tamsin was mad and crying.

"What's going on?" I asked.

Fiona filled me in. "They're fighting over who gets to marry Mark."

"Okay, this is ridiculous," I said, trying to drown out the insanity going on in front of me. "First of all, we're hardly old enough to get married. Second of all, Mark gets a vote. Has anyone gone upstairs to ask him what he thinks?"

Gasps of horror erupted around me.

"I didn't think so."

"So until he is consulted, and we are like twenty, I think this is all a moot point."

Poor Anita sniffled in the corner. "I'm sorry. I never meant to start a fight."

"You didn't," I said. "It's not your fault for liking him. He *is* very cute."

"Don't tell me you like him, too!" Sherise said.

I shook my head. "No, you all know I'm loyal to Andrew Finkel."

"Who asked about you after your lightning thing, remember?" Alex was always so encouraging. It was one of the many reasons why we were BFFs.

"Excuse me," Chuckles interrupted. "Will I get to go on soon?"

"Okay, so, can we all hug and make up? I have something that's going to scare the pants off all of you."

Alex gasped. "Are you . . . ?"

I nodded. "Go hug Tamsin," I said to her, needing us to get back to normal before I brought out the entertainment.

Alex complied, and then all the girls took their seats facing me. "Okay. So. Tamsin, I know it's your thirteenth birthday and all, but I thought it might be cool to have a clown come for your birthday party."

"A clown?" Sherise shrieked in laughter.

Tamsin groaned.

"No way, a clown?" Fiona asked, her eyebrows high up on her forehead. "Clowns are the lamest thing ever!"

"I like clowns," Anita said quietly.

"Well, watch this." I lifted up my arms and closed my eyes. "I wish there was an invisible clown here, and I wish he would make me a balloon animal!"

The girls all snickered.

I opened my eyes and then everyone gasped when a balloon appeared, suspended in the air right in front of us.

"Oh!"

The balloon filled with air and then magically started twisting on itself, turning into a dog.

"Lilah!" Tamsin hollered. "How are you doing that?"

"I'm going to faint," Anita said.

I looked at her. She was wide-eyed, but she looked okay. I didn't really think she would faint.

"How . . . what . . . wow!" Fiona was almost speechless.

Suddenly the dog bounced over to Tamsin, who reluctantly plucked it out of the air.

"For the birthday girl," I said.

"How did you do that?" she asked, looking up at me with awe and a little bit of fear in her eyes.

"It wasn't actually me," I said.

We all looked as another balloon, a yellow one, started inflating in front of us.

"I guess I should tell you girls about what happened to me when I got hit by lightning."

They looked from the balloon to me.

While Chuckles made us all balloon animals, I told the girls my story.

CHAPTER 10

The rest of Tamsin's party, after I swore the girls to complete and utter secrecy, was filled with me answering questions about my ability.

Could I predict the future? No.

Could I talk to anyone I wanted? Not to my knowledge—so far all the ghosts had come to me.

Could I make things move with my mind? I tried it on the Ouija board. A big nope on that.

Could I make people do things with my mind? I concentrated really hard on Alex, but she didn't cluck or strut around like a chicken, so no.

Could I make Andrew Finkel fall in love with me? Well, I was willing to try, but I doubted talking to spirits would help. And falling in love might be a bit of a long shot when he hadn't even asked me to go to the dance with him yet.

"But his father's dead. Maybe he can help you," Fiona suggested.

I never thought of that. But I wasn't so sure I wanted to go that route.

"I would love to talk to my son," a man said suddenly. It wasn't Chuckles, either; he had left when we got tired of the balloon animals.

My eyes went really wide.

"What?" Alex asked, obviously noticing my sudden change of expression.

"Who is there?" I asked, looking up at the ceiling.

"Jacob Finkel. I'm Andrew's dad."

I held my breath, not believing it.

"It's Andrew's father. He wants to talk to his son."

Tamsin squealed and clapped her hands. "Oh Lilah, this is perfect!"

I wasn't so sure. My stomach was doing flip-flops.

"Mr. Finkel?" I asked. "Do you have a special message for your son?"

There was a long pause and I thought maybe he'd left.

"I'd like to tell him I'm proud of him."

I blushed. It was a sweet message, but how was I going to tell Andrew that without dying of embarrassment?

"He's a nice boy," my grandmother said out of the blue.

"He has turned out well, hasn't he?" Mr. Finkel said.

"My Lilah has a crush on him."

"BUBBY!" I yelled. How embarrassing!

"Well, it's true!"

"Well, you don't have to tell his father that. *Sheesh!*"

Then I realized my friends were all staring at me with wide eyes. "My grandmother is telling Mr. Finkel all my secrets," I explained.

"Not all of them, Lilah. I didn't tell him about the time . . ."

"BUBBY!" I interrupted. "Please stop talking!"

She did, thankfully.

"I have a plan," Alex said. "We're going to get you together with Andrew. We're going to get him to ask you to go to the dance. And you're going to use your new medium abilities to do it."

I was terrified and excited all at the same time. If anyone could come up with a great plan, it was Alex.

When Alex said we were going to put a note in Andrew's locker, I didn't realize she meant we were going to be performing some sort of covert *Mission Impossible* exercise. After we spent most of Tuesday's lunch hour composing the cryptic note, we headed up to where Andrew's locker was.

The trick was getting the note into the locker without anyone seeing.

There were two ways we could go about it.

First, one of us could cause a big distraction, allowing the other access to the locker while everyone in the hall was busy checking out the commotion.

Or second, we could be late for third period and slip the note in when everyone else was already in class.

Alex volunteered for the former, but I thought the latter was the smarter choice. Although Alex loved a scene, it seemed best to be discreet.

Thankfully, Alex didn't put up much of a fight, so we spent the last few minutes of lunch in the bathroom pretending to fix our hair and makeup.

Once the bell rang, Alex and I waited a minute and then walked down the hall, pausing only long enough for her to slip the note through the vent at the top of Andrew's locker. I could only hope it landed in a very obvious spot, and that he saw it either at afternoon break or at the end of the day.

I wouldn't know for sure until later that night at the Beanery Café, the spot Alex and I picked as the perfect location to break it to Andrew Finkel that his father had a message from beyond.

CHAPTER II

Dad ate his noodle casserole as though he liked it. I knew it wasn't his favorite, but it was easy to throw together and was ready for when he got home, ensuring I'd be on time for my supersecret rendezvous with Andrew Finkel.

There was a lull in our "how was your day" conversation when I stopped eating to watch him shovel the food into his mouth. He ate like he'd never eaten before and didn't expect to again.

It was pretty gross.

"Dad?"

"Mmmhmm," he mumbled, not even looking up from his food. I wondered when he'd turned into a Neanderthal and how I'd never noticed before now.

"Dad!"

That got his attention. He put his fork down. "What is it?"

"Um, well, I don't mean to be . . . indelicate, but is that how you ate on your date?"

He looked down at his plate and then back up at me. "What do you mean?"

I cringed and looked down at my own plate, suddenly sorry I'd said anything. "Nothing."

"What is it?"

I took a breath and looked at him. "Well . . . you kind of look like a pig when you eat."

He didn't flinch when I said it, but he swallowed hard, his Adam's apple moving up and down in his neck.

"Sorry."

He waved me off, pretending he didn't care. "Don't be. I guess it's better I know, since I have another date this weekend."

I dropped my fork on my plate, causing a loud clatter. *"You do not!"*

Finally, Dad was smiling. "It's true."

"Oh, Dad, that is awesome!" I jumped up out of my chair and ran around the table to give him a big hug.

"Ugh!" Dad protested when I squeezed too hard. "Tell me *everything*."

"Let go of me, and I'll tell you."

Retracting my arms, I returned to my seat, awaiting the details.

Which oozed out of him like ketchup out of a glass bottle. It was totally maddening.

"Well, her name is Sharon," he said, then daintily scooped up a few noodles with his fork and deposited them in his mouth.

"Sharon what?"

While I waited for him to continue, Dad chewed in a very slow and precise manner. Okay, maybe it would have been better if I'd heard about his date *before* I criticized his sloppy eating habits.

Once every morsel of food was cleared from his mouth, he continued.

"Sharon Adler. You might have met her at the high holidays at temple. Her mother and your grandmother used to play bridge."

I fought a big smile, unwilling to arouse suspicion but knowing who was behind this setup. I had no idea how my dead grandmother had pulled it off, but I had no doubt she was behind it. "Oh, is her name Marjorie?"

"Yes, that's right—Marjorie Adler. Good memory!" He took another few noodles and continued. "It was strange, she phoned me out of the blue at work today."

Out of the blue, as if.

"Really? That's weird. Did she say why?"

He shook his head. "Not really. She just said she was recently divorced and had been thinking maybe we could get together."

I made a mental note to get the details from Bubby later.

"Anyway, you'll be very proud of me, Lilah. I asked her where she wanted to go and it turns out we both like Thai."

"I *am* proud of you, Dad. *Hugely* proud. And what are you going to wear?"

He took a deep breath. "How about you take your old man shopping Friday night so we can find something nice? My shirt from the other night is ruined and it's been a long time since I've bought new clothes."

"Of course I'll take you shopping! We'll get you some really hip clothes, maybe even some new threads for work."

Dad actually looked pleased. He dabbed at his mouth with his napkin, making a big show of his manners.

I applauded and then glanced at the clock: 6:17.

The note we'd left in Andrew Finkel's locker had said to meet us at the Beanery Café at seven. And I still needed some hair and makeup time.

"Sorry, but I've gotta run." Pushing my chair back from the table, I picked up my plate and put it in the sink. "Do you mind clearing tonight?"

"It's the least I can do for my *stylist*," he said, making me throw my arms around him again. He was a total nerd, but he was definitely a lovable nerd.

"Ugh. If you keep squeezing me like that, I'm going to throw up my dinner."

"Sorry, I'm just feeling a bit enthusiastic about your dating."

"Funny, I'm feeling a bit *nauseated* about my dating."

"Oh, don't worry," I said, finishing the last of my milk before putting the glass in the sink. "You'll do great this time. Just think. It can't be any worse than that last one."

Let's hope.

"Well, that's true," Dad said in a rare show of optimism.

"I'll see you later."

"Where're you off to?"

I swallowed and quickly blurted out: "Oh just to the Beanery to meet Alex." It wasn't even a lie. Alex would be there.

Dad had enough going on. I didn't need to tell him I was meeting a boy. And I especially didn't need to tell him I was meeting this boy to give him a message from his dead father.

Alex met me on the corner and we proceeded to the café. Understandably, I was nervous. Really nervous. I mean, it's not every day that you summon a hottie to meet you outside of school to tell him his dead father wants to talk to him. And even though it was easy to give my dad advice when it came to *my* love life, I really had no clue what I was doing.

"What if he doesn't show up?" I asked Alex.

"He'll show up." She seemed very sure of it. Which made my stomach do a big flip.

"What if he *does* show up?" I asked.

She stopped walking. "What is wrong with you, Lilah?"

I frowned. "He's very cute."

She shook her head. "And?"

"It's a little intimidating."

She started walking again. "You shouldn't be intimidated. Just remember you're legit."

"Huh?"

"You have a real reason to contact him. His father really wants to talk to him."

"That's true," a man, presumably Mr. Finkel, said.

Okay, so now I was embarrassed, discussing all of this with his father eavesdropping. "Can we please get some privacy?"

"Sorry."

Alex looked around. "Oh, you mean . . ."

"Yeah, Andrew's dad is already here."

"Oh."

We didn't talk for the final two blocks. I opened the door and we walked into the noisy café. There were sounds of espresso machines and cash registers and lots of people talking.

"What are you going to have?" I asked Alex.

"Iced cappuccino, you?"

"Just an Italian soda. But I'll buy. It's my treat today." I wouldn't normally splurge, but Dad had handed me a ten before I'd left the house.

Alex smiled and thanked me.

"Go get that table over there," I said, pointing to a small bistro table in the back.

She shuffled off and I turned to the barista to order.

"Oh look, it's cargo pants," I heard from behind me. I turned. Yep, because I had that kind of luck, it was Dolly Madison.

I wasn't even *wearing* my cargo pants. But either way, I ignored her and ordered drinks for me and Alex.

"Didn't you hear me?" she said.

I looked back at her. "I heard you. You didn't ask me a direct question, so I didn't think you were looking for a response."

That shut her up.

For about four seconds.

"Don't you know this is an eighth-grader hang-out?"

"Oh, I'm sorry," I said, trying hard not to sound sorry at all. "I must have missed the sign on the door."

Speaking of the door, at that second, it opened and Andrew Finkel came walking in. "Oh," I must have said out loud.

Dolly followed my gaze and looked toward the door.

"Oh, what is this, some kind of date?" she said really loud. Loud enough for Andrew to hear.

I blushed.

"NO! It's NOT a date," I said, looking at Andrew to make sure he knew I was really clear. His cheeks were red, too. Probably even redder than mine were.

He looked away. It was very cute.

"Six fifty," the barista said, bringing me back to reality. I paid for the drinks and took them from the counter.

"We're over here, Andrew," I managed to say without fainting before I turned to join Alex over at the table.

"What was that all about?" she asked as I put her iced cap in front of her.

"Dolly's being a meanie, as usual." I sat down, with my back deliberately to her and the counter so

I could compose myself before Andrew came and sat with us. I was a bundle of nerves.

"Don't look now," Alex said quietly. "But Dolly's making a move on your dude."

I couldn't help myself; I whipped my head around so fast, a muscle in my neck pulled. "Ow!"

"I told you not to look!" Alex hissed.

Here's the thing—you can't tell someone not to look and then drop a big bomb on them like Dolly Madison, older girl with boobs, is macking on your guy and then expect the other person to really not look. It's basically impossible, like telling someone to keep their eyes open when they sneeze. Nope, can't be done.

But as I massaged the cramped-up muscle in my neck, I watched as Dolly stood too close to Andrew and made a point of laughing loudly at something he said. She was totally flirting with him and probably just to be mean to me.

I turned back to Alex and exhaled loudly. "Maybe I should see if I can find someone who wouldn't mind haunting her for a while."

"Lilah," my grandmother said with a big cluck of her tongue. "That's not very nice."

Like Dolly was concerned about being nice to me? But no, of course I wouldn't ask some ghost to haunt her. I wasn't vengeful. That wasn't my style.

"Can you do that?" Alex asked. "Can you get someone to haunt her? Maybe undo her bra when she's in front of the whole school doing her eighth-grade speech?"

Of course, being vengeful *was* Alex's style.

I smiled. "No, I can't do that. But it's fun to think about, isn't it?"

"Hi, Lilah. Hi, Alex," Andrew said from just behind me.

I almost fell out of my chair.

"Hi, Andrew," Alex said, coming to my rescue. Then, she stood up and grabbed her drink. "I think I'll leave you two alone so you can chat."

NO! I thought. *This wasn't part of the plan!* But as I stared at my friend, hoping she would sit back down, she winked at me and left to go sit by herself at a different table. As I watched her go, I also got to see Dolly and her friends sit in a booth with a perfect view of our table. She sneered at me, so I quickly turned away.

"Have a seat," I croaked, pointing at Alex's recently vacated chair.

"Thanks."

I took a sip of my soda, buying a minute.

"So," he said, stirring the straw in whatever coffee-colored concoction it was he was drinking. The ice cubes clattered around noisily.

"So," I echoed.

He looked up at me. "Your note said this had to do with my dad?"

I looked down at my cup. "Yes. Um . . ."

"You know my dad died a few years ago, right?"

I nodded and then looked up at him. "That's why I needed to talk to you."

"I don't understand. Is someone in your family sick or something?"

"No. It's not like that . . ." I had to stop stalling and just get on with it.

"Tell him he looks good," Mr. Finkel said suddenly.

I took a breath. I couldn't open with a message. I had to ease Andrew in.

"Do you remember how I got hit by lightning?"

Andrew nodded. "Yeah. Are you okay? I mean, you look okay." Then he blushed, which was very cute.

"Yeah, I'm okay. I mean, more or less."

He opened his mouth to say something, but I put up my hand to stop him, needing to get my story out. "Well, since then, I have an ability . . . the ability to hear dead people."

His eyes went really wide and then he crossed his arms at his chest. "Come on, you do not."

"Really, I do. I can prove it."

He lifted his eyebrow—just the right one. "So prove it, then."

"Tell him you know he's wearing his Spider-Man boxer shorts."

I felt my face get really hot. "I can't say that!" I blurted out.

"Can't say what?" Andrew asked.

Oh, this is not going well, I thought.

"Okay, I see your point," Mr. Finkel said. "Tell him you know he had peanut butter on toast for breakfast."

"That's better."

"Who are you talking to?" Andrew asked, frowning.

"Your dad."

He pushed back in his chair and reached for his drink, looking like he was going to get up and leave.

"Wait," I said. "I can prove it. He says you had peanut butter on toast for breakfast."

"So? That's hardly proof."

"Tell him you know he just got new skates for his birthday."

"Oh," I said. "I didn't know it was your birthday. Your dad says you got new skates."

Andrew frowned. "That's still not proof. Everyone on my hockey team knows I got new skates."

He pushed back his chair again and really got up this time.

"Wait," I said, my voice squeaky.

His face scrunched up and his lip quivered a bit. "I don't know what kind of joke this is, Lilah, but it's not funny. My dad's dead. Okay? Not. Funny."

My heart was racing, and it was like my brain was melting. I couldn't think of what to say to make him believe me. "I know, but . . ."

"Tell him about the Spider-Man boxers," his dad said.

"I can't do that," I hissed at his father.

Andrew shook his head and turned to leave.

"Andrew! Wait!" I yelled as a last chance. "I know about your underwear!"

Funny, that just made him leave faster. And all I could do was watch in horror.

After he was out the door, I glanced at Dolly, who seemed to be having a seizure of some sort and I was about to jump up and help her until I realized she was laughing.

At me.

Like, killing herself over my humiliation.

"Uh, Lilah, what on earth was that?" Alex asked from beside me.

I looked up at my friend, who was slurping on her iced cap.

I fought the tears of anger and frustration that wanted desperately to leave my eyes. I couldn't cry and let Dolly see. After a deep breath, I said, "That, my friend Alex, was both the beginning and the bitter end of my career as a medium."

"Harsh," she said, the straw skidding along the bottom of her empty cup as she sucked up the last little bit of her drink.

"Shut it," I said. "This was your idea."

"*That,* whatever it was, was not my idea. And what was that about his underwear?"

I hid my face in my hands. "How am I supposed to go back to school? How am I supposed to face him in class now? Oh, Alex, what have I done? I never dreamed for a second that he wouldn't believe me."

"There, there," my grandmother said.

I lifted my head up and wiped at my eyes. "Oh *now* you show up, Bubby. Couldn't you have helped me?!"

"*Tsk,* Lilah, don't be mad at me. I can't do everything for you."

"Maybe the underwear thing was my fault," Mr. Finkel said. At least he sounded guilty.

"Ya think?" I said, and then sighed because it was too late to do anything about it now. "I ruined it, Bubby. What am I supposed to do now?"

"Don't worry, Lilah. It's not ruined. You'll just have to try again to convince him."

"And I promise, I won't bring up his underwear again," his father said.

I looked up at Alex.

"What?" she said, and I remembered that she couldn't hear the conversation going on around me.

"Never mind, let's get out of here." I got up and tossed the rest of my drink into the trash. I walked past Dolly, avoiding looking at her.

"That was smooth," she said.

I started to turn around, but Alex pushed me from behind toward the door.

"Not worth it," she said to me and then she hollered, "No one cares what Ding Dongs think, anyway! Oh wait, wrong snack cake, Ms. Dolly Madison!"

We both snickered as we bolted out of the café.

It didn't make up for the horror of everything, but at least I didn't die of embarrassment on the threshold of the café.

Thank you, Alex.

CHAPTER 12

Thursday. Math class. Makeup test. *Blech.*

And if that wasn't bad enough, I had to walk right past Andrew to get to my seat. I didn't look anywhere near him and managed to get to my chair without incident, although I felt my cheeks heat up terribly.

Because I yelled about his underwear in a public place.

Ugh, could anything be more humiliating?

The one good thing about having to make up the math test was that while everyone else got to work ahead in the module, I had to sit at the very back of the class by myself, which meant no chance of any communication between me and Andrew. I totally did not want to talk to him. Mostly. You know, unless it was for him to tell me he'd had a sudden bout of amnesia and had no idea what we even talked about at the café and then ask me to the upcoming seventh-grade dance. Although who was I trying to kid? That was never going to happen.

One crisis at a time—back to the dire situation at hand. I'd kind of hoped Mr. Burrows would have just assumed I'd already taken the test and had, of course, gotten it perfect, but no, he had a great memory and remembered quite clearly that I had not taken the test.

And I guess he probably knew there was no way I would ace it, because I'd never aced anything in math.

Especially when it had word problems, which just made my brain ache.

Take this one, for example:

Cindy has $45.00. She goes to the mall and buys lipstick and then she buys shampoo, which is half the price of the lipstick. She then spends half of what she has left on a purse, leaving her with $15.00. How much did the shampoo cost?
How much did the lipstick cost?

I mean, come on. The *real* problem here is what shade is the lipstick? And what season is it, because that will determine whether she is to wear a lipstick or a lip *gloss*. And is the purse leather? Because I'm not really sure how I feel about leather, you know, PETA-wise, but I do know that leather is way more expensive than the fake stuff, so I'm not even sure if Cindy really has enough to buy all these items.

"Please, like I will ever need to twist my brain like this," I mumbled as I doodled a purse in the margin of the test paper.

"Want the answer?" someone asked.

I looked around. No one was looking at me.

"Want the answer?" the voice asked again.

Did I want the answer? Suddenly, I was faced with an ethical dilemma. Of course I wanted the answer. But was it right to use my powers to cheat?

No, it absolutely was not. And even though it would be nice to get a hundred on a math test (for once), I would feel guilty and hate myself for having cheated.

"No, thank you," I said quietly. "I'll figure it out on my own."

"Fine, fail your test then. I was just trying to help."

"Who are you?" I asked. "You're very rude."

"Rufus. And I may be rude, but I'm rude with all the answers. I'm just trying to help you. Just like I wanted to help you haunt people, and I also helped you get back at Dolly in the bathroom."

"What do you mean?"

"You didn't think she fell all by herself, did you?"

I gasped, not liking this particular spirit at all. "That's not helping me! That's horrible! Please go away."

"Oh, come on, she wasn't really hurt. I was just having a little fun with her so she would leave you alone."

Even though he was trying to defend me, I didn't like this ghost's methods, and I didn't see how tripping someone was just "having a little fun." "I don't care. Please leave me alone."

"Good girl, Lilah," my grandmother said out of the blue.

"Who was that?"

"Just some mischievous young boy who doesn't seem to know right from wrong."

I shook my head.

"Now, Lilah, I think you need to get moving on that test. The period is almost over."

I groaned and returned to the problem at hand, wishing I was at the mall shopping instead of sitting in class just figuring out a problem about shopping.

Ironic, huh?

After math class (Mr. Burrows marked my test on the spot—I got a pass, although barely, but I was still kind of proud of myself for not cheating even though

I had the chance), I walked down the hall toward English when a sign on the wall grabbed my attention.

EIGHTH GRADE FASHION SHOW
PROCEEDS TO THE CANCER SOCIETY
$4–NEXT THURSDAY
7PM IN THE AUDITORIUM

Hmmm. That sounded like it would be fun. I kind of wished I was already in eighth grade so I could be involved.

Then I remembered that Andrew's father had passed away from cancer. Maybe if I helped out or sold a lot of tickets, he'd see that I really did care about him. And I'd be helping out a great cause so that maybe someday a kid like him wouldn't lose his dad. Or a great guy like Mr. Robertson wouldn't lose his girlfriend and bandmate.

Yes, that's a great idea, I thought, *I really want to help!*

"What are you looking at?" a voice said from behind me. I knew it wasn't a ghost. I turned to face Dolly Madison.

"I'm looking at a sign, it's not illegal."

"Don't bother coming to the fashion show," she said.

"Why? You can't stop me."

"It's only for the cool kids. Not kids who wear stupid cargo pants. Or yell out random things about guys' underwear."

I got really mad and wanted to punch her in the nose, but she was a lot taller than me, and I wasn't sure if I could reach. And it's not right to hit people. Oh, and I'm pretty sure she'd kick my butt.

So instead of punching her in the nose, I said. "You think you own the fashion show?"

"Uh, I'm running it, dork. So yeah, I do think I own the fashion show."

Okay, so that kind of backfired on me, but still, I said, "Well, I hope it's a total bomb and that you fall on your face. Although, of course, you'll have your humongous boobs to break your fall."

I heard sudden laughter and it sounded like a boy's, but I didn't have time to even think about it, because Dolly looked like she was getting ready to kill me. I turned and ran away from her as fast as I could—around the corner and into the bathroom— so she wouldn't catch me. When I was in a stall, I quickly realized I wasn't alone.

"I can help you," a boy's familiar voice said.

"Rufus?"

"The one and only."

"You shouldn't be in the girls' bathroom!"

"I'm dead, it doesn't matter. Do you want my help or not?"

"Help with what?"

"To get back at Dolly."

My stomach flip-flopped, but he definitely had my attention. "What do you mean? How? I don't want to hurt her."

"No, nothing like that. Why don't we give her a taste of her own medicine? She's not the only one who can be mean!"

I knew it probably wasn't a good idea, but I couldn't help myself when I asked, "What can we do?"

"You just wait and see!"

"Do you promise you won't hurt her?"

But then he was gone, and no amount of coaxing would get him to come back and tell me his plan. He did say he wouldn't trip her, right? He knew I wasn't into really hurting people. I hoped.

I couldn't wait to talk to Alex; I needed to tell her that we were SO going to that fashion show and we were going to make sure we sold a ton of tickets— that Dolly with her attitude and boobs was not going to stop me from doing *anything*. Especially now that I had the spirit world on my side.

"What do you think he's going to do?" Alex asked after class when we were at our lockers.

I shrugged. "He wouldn't say. What can a ghost do to a mean girl?"

Alex got a wicked look on her face. "I'm sure just about anything. I can't wait."

My stomach fluttered a little. "I hope he doesn't hurt her. You know, really hurt her. I told him not to, but he tripped her that time."

"Please," Alex said. "I thought you wanted revenge. Maybe he'll unhook her bra in class or spill some mashed potatoes on her in the cafeteria, or maybe . . . Oh, *shhhh*. Here comes Andrew!"

I wanted to jump into my locker and close the door. But I didn't and just turned away as Andrew walked up and started working on his lock.

"Hi, Andrew," Alex said. I could have killed her.

"Oh, uh, hi, Alex."

"Say hi to Andrew, Lilah." Now I *really* was going to kill her.

"Andrew's not talking to me, Alex," I hissed.

"Oh?" she said loudly. "Why is that, I wonder?"

Andrew slammed his locker closed. "Because she's a liar, that's why."

Right then, my heart broke open in two pieces. I would have run away if I thought my legs would have carried me.

Alex gasped and I knew it wasn't part of her act. "What?"

"She tried to tell me she's talked to my dad, my

dead dad. As if. It's a stupid, mean trick she's trying to play on me."

Tears escaped my eyes.

"It's no trick," Alex said. "She's for real."

"Whatever."

Alex turned to me. "Tell him; tell him something that will convince him."

I opened my mouth, but nothing came out.

"Oh, Lilah," my grandmother said. "His father's not around. I'm so sorry."

"Just leave me alone," Andrew said.

"Wait!" Alex said, grabbing his arm. She turned to me, "Lilah, say something."

I had nothing.

Andrew walked away.

CHAPTER 13

During lunch period on Friday, I was sitting alone in the cafeteria, eating my salad and wishing Alex didn't have an orthodontist appointment. The rest of our friends had gymnastics club and I hated eating alone, but Alex had said she'd probably be back by lunch and to wait for her, so there I sat.

"I'm glad to see you eating the salad today," a voice said from across the table, where no one sat.

"Thanks, Miss Marion," I said to the lunch lady spirit. "I figure salad's a safe bet. That chicken à la king looked gross."

"Indeed it did."

"Who're you talking to?" said another voice, from beside me.

Uh-oh. I looked up and there was Andrew Finkel, holding a lunch tray and staring at me with a funny look on his face.

"What's it to you?" I asked.

"Are you okay?"

"Why do you care? I'm just a big liar."

"Lilah." The way he said my name—kind of softly and not at all meanly—made me look up at him. "I didn't mean to call you a liar."

"Yes, you did."

He shook his head. "I just . . . I just saw you sitting here talking . . . and wanted to make sure you're okay."

Clearly he thought I was insane and probably needed to be carted off to the psych ward. I guess I couldn't blame him.

I took a breath and tried to get my heart to stop racing around in my chest. "Yeah, I'm okay. I was just talking to . . . to myself, I guess."

"Who's Miss Marion?"

Busted.

I looked around, but no one seemed to be paying attention to us. "She's a ghost, okay?" I whispered.

Andrew said nothing, just stared at me.

It made me a little mad. "You can leave if you want. If you think I'm telling stories or something. You asked, so I told you."

Instead of leaving, he sat down.

I dragged my fork through the salad on my plate, no longer hungry. But I couldn't bring myself to tell him to go away.

"Can you really see ghosts?" he whispered.

I shook my head, still looking down into the depths of my romaine. "No," I said. "I can't *see* them. I can only hear them."

"For real?"

I looked up at him. "Yes, for real. You think I'd make this up?"

He shrugged.

"Well, I'm not making it up. Since the lightning, something in my brain switched and I can hear dead people."

He swallowed and then started unwrapping his sandwich. "And you really talked to my dad?"

"Yeah."

"Can you maybe prove it? I mean, I don't . . . I'm not calling you a liar or anything, but . . ."

I couldn't help but think about his underwear and my face heated up. Suddenly my salad was really interesting again.

"I don't even know if your dad is here now," I said, keeping my head down.

"I'm here," Mr. Finkel said.

"Oh."

"What?" Andrew asked.

"He's here."

"Lilah, tell him about the time George ate the whole turkey. That ought to do it."

"Okay," I said, finally looking up into Andrew's eyes. He looked really freaked, but not mad this time. I took a breath. "I'm supposed to tell you something about George eating a whole turkey?"

Andrew laughed but then got really serious.

"Who's George?"

"My grandma's dog. He stole the whole Thanksgiving turkey off the counter, and by the time we realized it, he'd eaten pretty much the entire thing."

"That's funny."

He nodded, but he wasn't smiling.

"Are you really talking to him?" he asked, his voice suddenly very low.

"Yeah. He wanted me to tell you he's proud of you."

Andrew's face suddenly scrunched up and his eyes got all glassy. I could tell he was trying not to cry. Heck, *I* was trying not to cry. Especially in the middle of the cafeteria.

"Tell him he needs to pull up his socks in math and science."

"I think he wants you to work harder in math and science."

Andrew nodded. "Is . . ." He cleared his throat. "Is he okay?"

"I'm fine. I miss you, but I'm fine, Son."

"He says he misses you."

"And Mom?"

"Every day, Andy. I miss your mom every day. But you're doing a good job taking care of her."

I relayed the message, trying not to get all emotional. But it was hard. This was like the hardest conversation ever.

Andrew blinked and looked away.

I took a sip of my water to give him a minute.

"I miss him. Can you tell him I miss him?" Andrew said, still not looking at me.

"He can hear you," I said.

A tear started to roll down his cheek. He swiped it away with the back of his hand. "I don't really know what else to say."

I opened my mouth to offer a suggestion, but in that second, Mr. Finkel said, "Tell my son I love him. Tell him I miss him and that he and his mom are in my thoughts every minute of every day."

Despite my throat getting tight, I took another sip of my water and told Andrew what his father said.

"I love you, Dad," he whispered.

"Tell him I have to go, Lilah," Mr. Finkel said after a long, quiet minute.

I did. Andrew nodded.

"But, Lilah," Mr. Finkel said.

"Yes?"

"Andy likes you. I thought I should tell you. He'd probably be upset if he knew I told you that, though," he said, and I could even hear the smile in his voice.

I willed my face not to heat up and go red, but I knew it was no use.

"What did he say?" Andrew asked.

I shrugged and took another sip of my water. "Something about getting your skates sharpened and then he had to go. Oh hey, happy birthday, by the way. Sorry I missed it."

"Thanks," Andrew said. "It was a couple of weeks ago."

"How does it feel to be thirteen?"

He shook his head. "Not much different. I don't really feel any older."

"No?" That was kind of disappointing. I expected that my thirteenth birthday, the one my religion said propelled me into adulthood, would be significant. I mean, it's a milestone, so it should feel different, right?

"So, uh, I guess that's it then?" he asked, pushing back his chair, suddenly looking like he was anxious to get away from the table. And me.

Maybe his dad was wrong. Maybe he didn't like me.

Alex chose to show up at that exact moment. She looked from me to Andrew and back again. "Hey. Everything okay?"

Andrew stood up. "Yes. Uh, thanks, Lilah. Really."

"Oh," Alex said. "Did you just ask Lilah to the seventh-grade dance?"

WHAT? I looked at my friend, sending *SHUT UP* vibes to her with my brain.

Didn't work.

"Oh," Alex fake chuckled. "I thought when you were thanking her it was for agreeing to go with you to the dance. Because I know she would have said yes."

"Uh . . ." Andrew blushed and looked at me. His face was contorted like he smelled something bad. I hoped it wasn't me.

Alex looked at me and winked. Not so discreetly, either. I wondered if I could hire a ghost to strangle her. *Never mind*, I thought, *I'll do it myself.*

"Oh, well. I didn't ask . . ."

"That's too bad," Alex said, shaking her head.

Andrew looked at me, his green eyes almost sparkling. "But um . . . Lilah, if you'd like to go . . ."

"Go! Go with him!" My grandmother hollered so loud it made me jump.

Good thing I had a strong heart. *Sheesh.*

"I'd like that," I managed to say.

"You'll have a great time," Mr. Finkel said.

Oh, good grief. Who knew when it was time to start dating that I'd have my own peanut gallery making comments?

But I forced myself to focus on the important fact: I had a date!

Andrew smiled. Like really smiled, showing teeth and everything. Maybe his dad was right. Maybe he did like me. And wow, he was ten times cuter when he smiled like that.

"Great."

"Great," Alex said. "Now I'm going to be a third wheel. You think Tamsin's brother will go to a seventh-grade dance? Yeah, I didn't think so either."

Alex was clearly insane.

"Do you like Sean? He'll be there," Andrew suggested.

I looked at Alex, who had liked Sean for about a millisecond when they'd reached for the same tuna sandwich in the cafeteria. Their hands had even touched.

She nodded. "That would be cool." She said it all nonchalant, like she didn't care one way or another, but I could tell that on the inside she was squealing, just the same as I was. Because we were going on a double date to the dance with a couple of really cute boys.

"Well, I'd better go. Thanks again, Lilah. For you know . . ." He glanced over at Alex.

"You're welcome, Andrew."

"Hey, Lilah?"

"Yeah?"

He smiled again before he said, "You can call me Andy. All my close friends do."

I swear I almost fainted.

CHAPTER 14

Friday night, Dad and I headed to the mall to get him some new clothes. First we stopped for dinner at the Cheesecake Factory (their fried mac and cheese is my favorite!). Dad called it a date, which I thought was kind of sad, but I didn't say anything. I mean, he did have plans to go out with a woman on a real date, so I didn't need to make him feel weird about it.

After dinner, we went to Sears to look at suits. With the help of a really hip young saleslady, we got him three pairs of pants, two sport jackets, four ties, and six new shirts. I was kind of shocked at how willing he was to get a whole new wardrobe, but he obviously knew he was overdue.

When he moved into the underwear department,

it was my sign to exit. Some things you just don't need to help your dad buy.

"I need some socks, Dad," I said as I pointed to the other side of the store. "I'll be over there when you're done."

Dad smiled and nodded before returning to the racks of boxers.

So I went over to the ladies' department, and on the way, my grandmother decided to make an appearance.

"You did a good job with him, Lilah."

"Thanks," I said, trying not to be obvious; I was talking to a ghost, after all. "It wasn't *all* me."

"You have good taste, though."

I smiled at the compliment.

"What are you buying?"

"I need some socks."

"Lilah?"

"Yes?"

"I think it's time you started wearing a bra."

I stopped walking, even though I was only as far as the panty-hose section.

"What?"

"Lilah, I think it's time you started wearing a bra. You are developing into a young woman and . . ."

"Bubby!" I felt my face heat up.

"What is it?"

"I don't need one of those."

"Don't be embarrassed, every woman goes through changes in her body . . ."

I ducked behind a rack of slippers. "Bubby, please!"

"She's right, dear." I looked around, but surprise, surprise, there was no one else around.

"Who's there?"

"Prissy Lafontaine."

"Oh, hello, Prissy!" Bubby said, obviously thrilled that she now had a coconspirator.

"I need socks," I said, and headed over toward the socks.

"Hmmm."

I sighed. "What is it?"

"Your grandmother is right. It's time you started wearing foundation garments."

Great, more fashion advice from a couple of old ghosts. And what on earth is a *foundation garment*? Ugh.

"I'll get Mom to take me when she gets back from her honeymoon."

"Oh, pish-posh," Prissy said. "Before I became a designer, I worked in the intimates department at Macy's. I've fitted thousands of women for brassieres. You're in capable hands."

Bubby laughed. I wasn't quite as amused myself.

"It's okay, I'll wait for Mom."

"Lilah, really," Bubby said in that voice that meant she wasn't taking no for an answer. "We will help you. Now go into the intimates department, and we'll help you pick some out to try on."

Oh, this is so not happening, I thought. I mean, I was kind of excited about getting a bra, but I had always assumed it would have been one of those mother-daughter bonding moments, not a dead grandmother–granddaughter–dead-fashion-icon bonding moment.

With another big sigh, I made my way over to the bra section and the fun *really* began. While I tried not to look like a psychotic preteen talking to herself, I managed to pick out three bras. I took them over to the lady behind the cash register and asked if I could try them on. She smiled down at me like I was four years old and asked if I wanted her to measure me for the bras. I politely declined and watched in horror as she took them out of the boxes and then handed them back to me.

"Here you go; I checked the sizes for you."

Gee, thanks.

I locked myself in one of the fitting rooms and took a deep breath. A little self-conscious, knowing my two ghostly bra stylists were watching, I took off my shirt and tried on the first bra. I barely had the thing on before I heard my name.

"Now who?"

"Is there a Lilah in here?" It was the saleslady and not another ghost.

"Oh, *I'm* Lilah."

"Your father is outside. He wanted me to let you know he's here."

Perfect. "Thank you."

After much complicated twisting and contorting and much discussion over underwire versus no underwire (I was strongly anti-underwire), I managed to try on all three bras and the consensus was that the second one looked best. Bubby suggested I get two for now until my breasts "decide what size they want to be" (yikes).

When I came out of the dressing room, the woman was standing there. "So, how did we do?"

"Well *I* did just fine," I said. "I'd like this one and another just like it, please."

"Get one in the blush pink," Prissy said. "You'll be glad you did."

I asked the lady for the second one in pink. I had no idea why, I was just not in the mood for an argument with a ghost.

"I'll be right back," she said.

I followed her out into the store and there was Dad, weighed down with numerous bags, grinning and blushing. *Ew.* I may as well have asked him to buy me a box of pads. How embarrassing. There are definitely some downsides to living with your dad when you're a *developing* twelve-year-old girl.

"Don't be embarrassed, Lilah," Bubby said, probably seeing how red my face was. "When your father was your age, I had to help him with his . . ."

"STOP!" I said as loud as I could without dad hearing. I SO did not want to hear embarrassing childhood stories about my dad. Especially when he was three feet in front of me. In the bra department of Sears. This was horrifying enough, thank you very much.

"Got what you need?" he asked, making no mention of the socks I had said I was looking for.

"Yep," I said, and led him over to the sales desk so he could pay. Without another word, he pulled out his credit card and paid for the bras while I wondered if everyone would know at school that I was now a member of the bra-wearing society. Not that it was an official society or anything, but girls who wore bras were different, more grown up, even the ones like me who barely had anything to put in them.

We were almost clear, almost at the door to the outside when I heard, "Hi, Lilah."

Like I was on TV, in slow motion, I turned to see Andrew (*eh-hem*, Andy) Finkel standing right there in front of me. He was smiling. I wondered if he could see through my bag to the bras inside. I put the bag behind my back, but instead of hiding it, I knocked it into my dad's arm, and it fell from my grasp.

And of course, because I hadn't been humiliated enough, the boxes slipped out and my size 32AA bras, one in white, one in blush pink, went sliding across the floor.

I truly wanted to die.

Dad was so laden with his bags that he couldn't bend down, but Andy, Mr. Polite and helpful, immediately bent down to help.

"I'VE GOT IT!" I hollered, and dropped to the floor to pick up the boxes as quickly as humanly possible. I stuffed them into the bag as I yelled, "I gotta go. Bye!"

And then, not even waiting to see if Dad would follow, I bolted from the store.

I'd *never* been so humiliated in all my life. NEVER!

Finally, Dad got close enough to the car to unlock it with the remote. I opened the door and dove inside, just in case Andrew (I couldn't bear to call him Andy after he'd seen my bras) came out of the store.

"Who was that?" Dad asked about a hundred hours later after he hung up his new clothes on the hook in the back and finally got into the driver's seat.

"Nobody."

"It didn't look like nobody."

"Just a guy from my school."

"A special guy?"

I gave Dad a look. It didn't work to get him to stop bugging me about it.

"Come on, Lilah, you can tell me."

"Just a guy, okay?"

He held up his hands, palms facing me. "Okay, I see this is a touchy subject with you."

Ya think? I thought, but I didn't say anything out loud.

"His mother seemed very nice."

"His *mother*?" I hadn't even noticed Andrew wasn't alone.

"Well yes, Lilah, after you ran out of there, I had to say *something*, so I introduced myself to his mother."

Oy, as my bubby would say.

"She was wearing a lovely suit. How could you not notice?" Ms. Lafontaine asked.

Oy again. "I was a little preoccupied," I said.

"What?" Dad looked over at me while he started the car.

"Nothing."

"Listen, Lilah," Dad said in his *you're about to get some fatherly advice, whether you want it or not* voice. "You have no reason to be embarrassed. All girls go through changes." He coughed, a sure sign *he* was embarrassed.

"Dad, I've already had this talk with Mom." And now with my dead grandmother *and* some old fashion designer who talks about things like *foundation garments* (and by the way, looking around the store, I didn't see even one sign for foundation garments, so I still have no idea what they are).

"Okay, kid, but remember, if you need to talk about anything, anything at all, I'm here."

"Sure," I said. But I didn't mean it. You can't talk to your dad about boobs and bras. No way.

CHAPTER 15

D ad left the house at six thirty. Twenty minutes later, Alex got dropped off so we could watch the rest of *Ghostbusters*, which we never got a chance to finish on our previous movie night.

As we grabbed some snacks from the kitchen and walked into the den, I told Alex about the bra disaster. She was sympathetic and groaned at all the right places in my story. Finally, someone who understood real humiliation!

"How did he look when he saw the bras?" she asked.

I shrugged. "I'm not sure. I was so completely mortified, I had to bolt."

"That's too bad. It would have been helpful to know if he was impressed." She rolled her eyes. "What am I saying? Of course he was impressed."

"Impressed? I'm not so sure."

Alex waved me off. "So, are you wearing one now?"

I nodded.

"Let's see."

Being that Alex is my BFF and we change next to each other for gym class, I wasn't at all embarrassed, so I pulled up my shirt to show her my bra. It was the blush pink one.

She cocked her head as she stared at my chest. "Not bad. But you need more to fill it."

"Like I have any control over that?"

Alex started flapping her arms like a chicken. "What about exercises?"

I pointed toward her still-flat chest. "They don't seem to be working for you any."

"True." She sighed and dropped to the couch. "I can't wait until we turn thirteen. It's all going to happen for us in eighth grade."

I nodded. "Thirteen will be special. Twelve is so blah." I grabbed the remote and started the movie while Alex jumped up and turned out the light.

"I know," Alex said. "But you never know, the dance is coming up."

I had completely forgotten! The seventh-grade dance. The one I was supposed to be going to with Andrew.

"I can't go."

Alex looked at me so fast, it was a surprise she didn't give herself whiplash. "What? You *have* to go."

"I can't go *now*."

"Why not?"

And here I thought Alex really got it. "Um, Alex, bra disaster?"

She waved me off again. "You watch, I bet he likes you more now that he knows you wear a bra."

I seriously doubted it. But I didn't want to talk about it anymore. I stuffed a handful of chips into my mouth and started the movie.

A few hours later, after Alex's parents showed up to take her home, I was vegging on the couch watching a repeat of *ANTM* (Cycle 10, one of my faves) when I heard Dad come home.

And I didn't need my dead grandmother to tell me it was another horrible date. It was written all over Dad's face.

"Oh no," I said, muting the TV.

"'Oh no' is right," said Bubby, who'd obviously chaperoned.

Dad dropped heavily onto the couch beside me.

"I think I'm done with dating, kid."

"What happened?"

He sighed and rubbed his temple before telling

me the following, "Well, I guess she's newly divorced. As in *very* newly divorced."

"And?"

He took a deep breath. "I thought I was being smart by letting her pick the restaurant, but what she didn't tell me was that it was the restaurant she and her ex-husband used to go to."

"That's weird, isn't it?"

"That's not the half of it," Bubby said.

"That's not the half of it," Dad said, almost at the same time. "She got sad about it and started talking all about her ex-husband and why he left her."

"Why did he leave her?" I asked.

Dad looked at me and shook his head. "Doesn't matter."

Bubby was much more helpful. "His receptionist."

Ah.

"Anyway, she was all weepy at the table, which was really uncomfortable, but then her ex actually came into the restaurant with his new girlfriend."

Bubby provided more pertinent details. "Who's half her age and twice her cup size."

Oh!

"Dad, I'm really sorry."

He looked up at me. "It's okay. I'm just not cut out for the dating scene."

I was suddenly very sad for him.

"Poor Martin," Bubby said, obviously feeling as bad for Dad as I was.

"What about eHarmony?"

He cocked his head and looked at me through narrowed eyes. "What do you know about eHarmony?"

I rolled my eyes. "Dad, I'm twelve. Trust me, I'm not on the Internet trolling for a husband. I see it all over the TV." And on cue, one of those sappy commercials with the nauseatingly happy couples popped on the screen.

Dad cringed. "I think I'm done for now."

"Oy," Bubby said with a sigh. "He'll never get married again."

I nodded. "I know."

"You know *what*?" Dad asked.

Oops.

"I mean . . . I know you need a break for now, but maybe in a bit you can try one of those websites. I don't want you to be lonely."

He put his arm around my shoulders. "As long as I've got you, I'm not lonely."

Something in his voice told me he wasn't being completely honest. He was *totally* lonely. He knew it, my grandmother knew it, and I knew it.

But what to do?

CHAPTER 16

Returning to school on Monday was terrifying, not just because I was wearing one of my new bras (the white one), but because Andrew was there and KNEW I was wearing one of my new bras.

I tried not to look at him at all during first period, but it was hard not to. I mean, there was the matter of his cuteness AND there was still that thing about going to the dance. Were we or weren't we? Alex of course wanted to go (because Sean was going to be her kind-of date), but I wasn't so sure going with Andrew was still on the table. Even if he wasn't deterred by my new bra-wearing status, I'd acted like a freak at the mall, and there was a good chance he wasn't into going to the dance with a crazy person.

But then the bell rang and before I could get out

of the classroom, he was there standing right next to me.

"Hi, Lilah," he said.

"Hi, Andre . . . Andy," I said back, feeling weird about calling him Andy, but he'd told me to. My heart fluttered a little.

"I'm looking forward to going to the dance on Friday," he said.

I looked up at him, but his eyes were on my chest. OMG!

Then I heard a voice, not a real voice or even a ghost's voice but a little voice in my head that sounded a lot like Alex. *He's impressed because he knows you're wearing a bra.*

"Eyes up, Son," Mr. Finkel said, sounding embarrassed.

My face heated up.

But then before it got really weird, Andy looked into my eyes. And his face got all red and splotchy. "Oh, uh, so Friday?"

"Friday," I said. Because I didn't know what else to say.

"I can get my mom to pick you up on our way."

I shook my head. "It's okay, I can meet you here." But then I thought maybe not accepting the ride would make it seem like I didn't really want to go with him. "Or, you can pick me up. Whatever, you know."

He looked confused. "Which would you prefer?"

"I . . . uh . . ."

"Lilah," my grandmother said out of the blue. "Tell him your father will want to drive you and that you'll meet him at the dance."

Grateful for the coaching, I said exactly that and exhaled when Andy smiled.

"Okay," he said.

"Great," I said.

"Great," he repeated.

I picked up my backpack. "I gotta go."

"Okay, bye, Lilah."

Before I could fumble and embarrass myself again, I got out of there.

The second I was out in the hall, Alex, Tamsin, Anita, Sherise, and Fiona swarmed around me and then dragged me into the bathroom and into a stall so we could talk semiprivately. It was pretty crowded, but we squished in.

"You're still going to the dance, right?" Alex asked.

I nodded.

Tamsin squealed.

Fiona had other things on her mind. "Show us your bra."

I pulled up my shirt.

"Oh, it's pretty," Anita said.

"Thanks. My grandmother and Priscilla Lafontaine helped me pick it out."

Fiona said, "Ohhh! Prissy Lafontaine? How cool is that?"

"I know," I said, suddenly feeling pretty good about my bra-buying experience. I'd never heard of Prissy Lafontaine before, but that my friends knew who she was, and that she seemed to like hanging around me, was pretty darn cool.

"Maybe she can help the rest of us," Anita said.

Alex looked Anita up and down. "You don't need a bra."

Anita pouted, but I said, "She needs one as much as I do," which I think made Anita feel better, even if it was a bit of a white lie.

The bell rang, signaling the end of break. The girls rushed out of the bathroom, but I still had to pee so I stayed behind, risking Mr. Burrows being a little upset at my tardiness.

Afterward, as I was drying my hands, I heard a strange noise. I froze. Then I heard it again; it was someone crying.

"Hello?" I said.

No response.

"Are you okay?"

"Go away," the girl said, sniffling.

I was undeterred. "What's the matter?"

"Just go away, okay?"

I recognized the voice. It was Dolly. I stood there for a second, not sure what to do. I mean, my instinct was to help, but it was *Dolly*.

She kept on crying and I was thinking about leaving when finally the stall door opened. Her face was all red and blotchy. I was going to leave, but instead I handed her a paper towel.

"The fashion show is going to be a complete failure," she said through her tears. "I'm going to have to cancel it. Some fund-raiser that turned out to be!"

"What? Why?" And why are you telling *me* this? I wanted to say.

"A bunch of the eighth-grade home-ec students bailed out on me for all sorts of ridiculous reasons. The dress rehearsal is on Wednesday, and nothing will be ready! Oh, I'm *such* a failure!"

"Uh, you're welcome, Lilah," a voice said. A voice that sounded a lot like Rufus's. "I told you revenge would be awesome!"

"You did this?" I whispered while Dolly sobbed into her paper towel.

"Yeah, you wanted me to. You wanted to get back at her," he said.

He was right. I *did* want to get back at Dolly. But I didn't want it like this. I didn't want the whole fashion show to be a failure.

And now, looking at Dolly crying, I realized I really didn't want to hurt her either. And ruining the fashion show was hurting her way more than tripping her in the bathroom. I never should have listened to Rufus.

"Go away," I said as quietly as I could.

"No," he said. "You wanted my help and I helped!"

"That was not helping! And I really want this fashion show to be successful!" I said, trying to be discreet.

"Oh, a *fashion show*. Everyone cares about their stupid *fashion show*. No one cares about me! Well, I'll show you and your stupid fashion show!"

"Rufus?!"

But there was nothing but silence: he was gone.

Oh no, I thought. *What have I done?*

Dolly sniffled, bringing me back to the current crisis. I put my hand on her arm. "What can I do to help?"

She looked at me. "Really?"

I nodded. "Of course."

She frowned. "After all I"—hiccup—"said to you?"

I swallowed my own guilt over what *I* did to *her* and figured we were probably even. I nodded again. "Yes."

"That's so nice of you. Are you sure?"

I'm not as nice as you think I am, I thought. "Of course I'll help."

She sniffled a couple more times and then said, "Can you sew?"

I opened my mouth to say no, but Ms. Lafontaine hollered out, "I CAN!"

"That doesn't help us," I said.

"What?" Dolly asked.

"Oh, uh . . . ," I stammered, not really sure if I should tell Dolly about my "abilities."

But Ms. Lafontaine was not to be stopped. "I can sew, Lilah. I can help with the designs."

"Dolly," I said, looking straight into her eyes so she knew I was serious. "I want to help you, but I have to get to math class right now. Meet me in the cafeteria at lunch and I will explain everything and we'll figure it out."

She took a deep breath. "Thank you so much, Lilah. And I'm so sorry for being mean to you." She looked down at the tattered paper towel in her hands. "I really am sorry."

I patted her arm. "It's okay, we'll figure it out. But right now, I gotta go."

She nodded and then before I was superlate, I ran out of there.

As I sat in math class, zoning out instead of working on the fractions that were on the board (ugh, WHO, please tell me, WHO can stand fractions?), I heard my name. Looking around, I realized it was Ms. Lafontaine.

"What?" I said softly.

"I am so excited to help you and your friends!"

The class was so quiet, it was going to be hard to have a conversation, so I wrote in my notebook:

How are you going to help?

"Well, maybe we can try something," she said.

Like what?

"Maybe . . . Perhaps I can use your body."

"No way," my grandmother said so loudly that I jumped in my chair.

Mr. Burrows looked up at me.

"Leg cramp," I said, cringing.

"But Dora, it's the only way to get all the outfits done in time. Lilah said herself she can't sew."

Home ec isn't until eighth grade.

"I don't want you messing with her body," Bubby said in her *and that's that* tone.

"But how else can we get all the work done?" Ms. Lafontaine had a very good point.

I'm willing to try it.

"Not a chance," Bubby said.

My body, my choice. I need to make it up to Dolly. And I need for the show to be awesome and make a ton of money.

"I won't go against your grandmother's wishes," said Ms. Lafontaine.

Bubby, please. It's the only way.

After several long moments, she finally agreed. "We will try it tonight, but if any harm comes to her, I'm calling it off."

"That's fair," Ms. Lafontaine said. "Lilah, are you sure?"

I nodded. "Yeah, I am," I said out loud, relieved. And terrified!

CHAPTER 17

At lunch, while we ate (Miss Marion gave the chicken fingers the all clear), I filled Dolly in on my being a medium. Alex and the rest of the girls attested to the truth in my story. I would have proved it, but the cafeteria was noisy and a bit too public.

"So how are you going to help?" Dolly asked.

"We're going to try to let Priscilla Lafontaine take over my body so that I can help you sew all the outfits."

Everyone at the table gasped. Understandably.

"Wait," Dolly said suspiciously. "Prissy Lafontaine? The mega-super-famous fashion designer?"

"Yep, the one and only!"

Dolly sat back in her chair. "Wow, she's like . . . huge."

"You can do that?" Fiona asked. "You can let her take over your body?"

"That's scary," Anita said, looking like she'd just eaten a bug.

"We're going to try. What other choice do we have?" I asked Dolly.

She shook her head. "None. I hope it works."

"Me, too," I said, trying not to let on how scared I was.

"What about my model shortage?"

I looked around the table. "We can all model."

Dolly smiled and looked at everyone. "You'd all do that? For me?"

"Sure," Alex said. "That would be cool. We all want to *be* models, so it will be perfect, right girls?"

Everyone agreed.

Dolly's eyes got all glassy, but before she could start weeping from gratitude, I asked her about the clothes. "Oh!" she said, opening her backpack. "I have sketches here." She pulled out a big sketch pad and started showing us her designs.

"Not bad," Ms. Lafontaine said. "Not bad at all. This girl has talent."

I relayed the message to Dolly. She swallowed hard and had to dab at her eyes, but I could tell she was happy and who could blame her? "Thank you," she said. "Please, Lilah, tell her thank you for me."

I smiled at Dolly. "She heard you."

It was going to all fall into place, just as long as I could become possessed and sew high-fashion outfits. Oh, and in two days!

Yep, no problem. Gulp!

Bubby said we couldn't try the possession thing unless it was at my house in case anything went wrong, so Alex and Dolly came home with me and we went right up to my room. Dad wasn't home yet, which was probably a good thing.

"Okay, let's give it a shot," I said, taking a deep breath.

"You should sit down," Alex suggested, pointing at my bed.

"Good idea."

I grabbed a pad and a pen off my desk and sat on the bed. I turned to an empty page. "Okay, Prissy, if you can take over my body, you can maybe try to write something."

"Okay," Ms. Lafontaine said. "Just try to relax and that will make it easier."

"Lilah," my grandmother said, sounding anxious. "You let me know if you are uncomfortable in any way, okay?"

"I will," I said.

I took a deep breath and closed my eyes.

CHAPTER 18

When I opened my eyes, I was surprised to see Alex and Dolly sitting on my bed staring at me. Then I remembered what we'd been trying to do. I felt like I must have zoned out for a little while I waited for Ms. Lafontaine to take over.

"Sorry, I guess we won't be able to sew all the outfits, after all."

Dolly blinked, her eyes all wide.

Alex did a double take. "Are you freaking kidding?"

My head ached a bit, so I rubbed my temple. "Kidding? What?"

"Lilah, look at this!" She held up the pad I'd grabbed off my desk. It was full of sketches of models and dresses, *very intricate* sketches. The kind I'd never have been able to make on my own.

"I did that?" I asked, taking the pad from Alex.

"Well, technically, we did it together," Prissy said, her voice full of pride.

"Wow!" I was flabbergasted. "So if I can draw, I can sew."

"We can!"

Dolly clapped her hands and then before I knew it, she threw her arms around me. "Oh, thank you, Lilah! Thank you so much!"

"You're welcome," I said. Then it was time to get to business. "Okay, girls, we have a lot of work to do. We should really get started."

As it turned out I—while possessed by the ghost of the person I now realized was a fashion GODDESS—was a pretty good sewer, although I was never actually conscious while sewing. It was pretty amazing to "wake up" after a long session at Dolly's sewing machine to see beautiful dresses that seemed to have just appeared. The only evidence that I even had anything to do with it was some aching in my hands.

I opted out of being a model, but with Anita, Fiona, Sherise, Tamsin, and even Alex helping out along with some of the eighth-grade girls, Dolly was fine without me. And anyway, it was probably best if I remained backstage with Ms. Lafontaine to help organize.

So the dress rehearsal *should* have gone fine. But when the girls started tripping as they walked down the catwalk, I knew something was up. Something otherworldly.

"Rufus! Stop whatever you're doing!"

The only response I got was him laughing.

I failed to see the humor in him ruining the fashion show and maybe even hurting one of the models.

"Stop it! This isn't about you!" I said. "Stop being such a rotten little boy!"

Just then, one of the big prop walls fell over, just missing Sherise and causing a loud BANG! Anita yelped and almost fell off the stage.

"Ha! This is so fun!" Rufus said. "I can't wait until the real show."

I couldn't believe this was happening. Dolly came running out from backstage. "What's going on?"

"We have a problem," I said.

"What do you mean?" she asked.

I looked around at all the girls. "It seems this fashion show is haunted."

A squeak erupted from Anita. Everyone else gasped.

"Bubby? Can you get rid of him?"

"Sorry, Lilah, you asked him for his help before—this is your problem, you're going to have to solve it."

I must admit, I was disappointed, but Bubby was probably right. In enlisting Rufus in the first place, I was getting what I deserved. But that didn't mean I couldn't try to fix it.

I just had to figure out how.

"Are you sure you're going to be able to fix this?" Dolly asked as we were hanging up the clothes after the rehearsal disaster.

"Trust me, I've got it all figured out," I said. It was a total lie. I had no idea what I was going to do. But this mess was all my fault; it was up to me to unhaunt the fashion show and make sure it was a success.

"I hope we sell more tickets at the door," Dolly said, thankfully changing the subject. "I've only sold about fifty so far."

"My dad sold a bunch at his job, and my mom even sent me an e-mail money transfer for two, even though she's on her honeymoon and can't come. But I think all the girls are bringing their parents. I'll even bring my dad." Who wasn't at all into fashion, but said he would come because he saw it was important to me.

"Thanks," Dolly said, smiling at me. I was so glad that we'd found a reason to be friends. When she wasn't being mean, Dolly was pretty nice.

"And I'll make announcements in all my classes and maybe more people will come." I'd already told Andy about the show; he'd seemed impressed and really liked that it was a fund-raiser for cancer research. He said he'd bring his mom, too, but it couldn't hurt to tell even more people.

"That's a good idea."

I nodded, hanging the last of the dresses. With a big exhale, I said. "Okay, I think that's it. I'm going to go home now."

"Lilah?" Dolly said.

"Yeah?"

"Can you please thank Ms. Lafontaine? I couldn't have done any of this without both you and her."

Her eyes filled up, which made mine do the same.

I cocked my head, waiting for a response from Prissy. "She's quiet," I said. "I bet she's resting up. She's had a busy couple of days."

"She *is* resting," my grandmother said. "She's exhausted, but in a good way. You girls have given her a wonderful gift. She so appreciates being able to help out and be useful. If she were here, she would thank both of you."

I relayed the message to Dolly. She smiled.

I gave her a hug and then went home to figure out how to get rid of that rotten little ghost, Rufus.

CHAPTER 19

All through dinner, I tried to figure out how to get rid of Rufus, or at least talk some sense into him, but I came up blank no matter how hard I thought about it.

"What's wrong, kiddo?" Dad asked.

I looked up. "What?"

"You sighed, like you're sad about something."

"Oh, just having some problems with a brat at school." Which was the truth. Dad didn't need to know the brat was dead.

"That boy from the mall?"

My face heated up. I looked down at my chicken. "No. Just a boy who is being a rotten pain in the butt."

"Ah, I see."

"What does that mean?"

"Well, kiddo, you don't have any brothers, so let me give you a hint about bratty boys. Usually, they are brats because they want attention."

"Even if it makes people mad and not like them?"

Dad nodded. "Sometimes even negative attention is better than no attention."

"Hmmm." I thought about what Rufus had said about nobody caring about him, and it suddenly made total sense that he was acting out to get attention. I picked up my plate and put it on the counter. "Thanks, Dad. I've got to go do some homework."

I got to my computer and googled Rufus along with my school's name. Bingo. There was a news story about him that even had a picture.

"Huh, he was bald," I said out loud.

"From the treatment," Rufus said suddenly. He would have scared me to death if his voice hadn't been so soft and sad.

"I'm sorry, Rufus."

He didn't say anything, so I read the article. "Leukemia—that's cancer, right?"

"Yeah."

"Why would you want to sabotage a fund-raiser for cancer research?"

"I'm dead, what do I care?"

"Well . . . for other kids. You know, so they don't have to go through what you did."

There was a long pause before he said, "I guess."

"Rufus, please. Let us have the fashion show; it's the right thing to do."

"Can I haunt the dance, then?"

My stomach flipped just thinking about the dance. "Uh, I'd really prefer you didn't!"

"Okay. I guess I won't. It's kind of nice hanging out with you, Lilah. I don't really have any friends anymore. They've all grown up and forgotten me."

That made me sad.

But also gave me an idea.

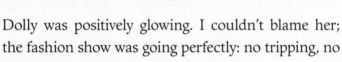

Dolly was positively glowing. I couldn't blame her; the fashion show was going perfectly: no tripping, no props falling, no problems whatsoever.

And, thanks, I'm sure, to the marketing efforts of me and my friends, the audience was almost packed. As I peeked out from behind the curtain on the left side of the stage, I saw a sea of faces, both of students and parents.

And it felt pretty good knowing that the money was going to a very good cause, too. Not only was I helping out Dolly, but by ensuring the success of the fashion show, I was helping out with the Cancer Society's fund-raising efforts, maybe helping them to cure cancer someday.

I glanced over to where Dad was sitting. I had sat down with him when we'd arrived but quickly went backstage to help out after he got settled among the sea of empty seats (I had to be there early).

Of course, I felt kind of bad just dumping him at a fashion show (not his cup of tea, as my grandmother used to, er, *still* says), but as I searched through the crowd, I found something quite amazing.

He was smiling and talking to someone who was sitting beside him.

Not just someone, but *a woman*.

"Who is that woman?"

"Your beau's mother," Bubby said.

"What?"

"Look who's sitting beside her."

Sure enough, on the other side of the woman was Andy, sitting there, fiddling with his cell phone.

Wow! It was like Dad was having an actual normal conversation with a woman.

"What are they talking about?"

"You starting to wear a bra."

My stomach rolled. "They are not. Please tell me they aren't."

"They are. Your father is concerned about you. He hopes you're not missing out because you live with him and not your mother. He knew you were embarrassed at Sears. He doesn't know you have us."

That made me sad. "I'm not missing out, Dad," I said, even though he couldn't hear me. Then, a mortifying thought occurred to me. "Andy's not listening, is he?"

Like it wasn't enough he was *there* for the original Brastock.

"No, he's playing a game on his thingamajig."

Thank goodness.

"No, he's not," said a man who sounded a lot like Andy's father.

"What is he doing?" I asked.

"He's sending a message to his friend Sean about the dance tomorrow night."

The dance! With all the drama around the fashion show, I'd all but forgotten the dance was tomorrow!

I hadn't even picked out what I was going to wear or anything.

My heart fluttered just thinking about it.

"Lilah! I need you!" Dolly said from the dressing area.

I took a last glance at my dad, who looked like he was having a really good time chatting with Andy's mom. Maybe, just maybe . . .

But what about Andy's dad? Wasn't that weird for him?

"Mr. Finkel?"

"Yes?"

"Are you okay if . . ." I didn't know how to say it. It was just too odd.

"I'm gone, Lilah," which sounded weird, because he was right there talking to me. "I just want her to be happy."

I nodded. It was kind of like what Bubby had said about my grandfather having a new girlfriend. I guess when you're dead, you just want your family to go on living.

"Lilah! Where are you? Alex's hem needs tacking!"

"You'd better go," Bubby said.

I nodded. "Keep an eye on them, Bubby. I want a full report later."

The fashion show was a smashing success, and not just because it went off perfectly, and not just because we raised a TON of money. Not just because we dedicated the show to Rufus Moore, the young student who'd died of leukemia a decade before. And not just because all my friends were totally fierce on the runway, doing their best *ANTM* struts in the clothes I had sewn. But because Dad left there with a big smirk on his face (the kind I'd never seen on him before, but I *knew* it was the smile of the smitten) and Andy's mom's cell number in his pocket. It was a bit weird that it was Andy's mom, but still, I was glad he was making progress.

He didn't tell me about the phone number, but hey, I'm a medium, I have my sources.

And my sources couldn't have been more pleased. "He's going out with her, Lilah! Do you believe it?" Bubby said as we were in the car on the way home. It was about the thousandth time she'd said it, too. I was getting a little annoyed. But it's not like I could tell her to shut it, I mean, Dad was right beside me.

"So," I said. "Tomorrow night is the seventh-grade dance."

Dad glanced over. "I know. You said you wanted me to drive you, right?"

He had plans to meet up with Rachel, Andy's mom, for coffee after they each dropped us off. *He* hadn't told me, but again, *sources*.

"Yeah," I said. Then I got to feeling a bit mischievous. "What are you going to do while I'm at the dance?"

He looked over at me again. He wanted to tell me, it was obvious. But there was something holding him back.

"He doesn't want to embarrass you," Bubby said. "Her son is in your class. He doesn't want to make things weird for you."

Aw, how considerate! But I wondered if Dad knew about me and Andy going to the dance together.

"I'm meeting a friend for coffee," was all he said.

I didn't push him to tell me who his "friend" was.

And I did wonder if Andy knew what had been going on right beside him or if he'd been too intent on texting Sean about the dance. I wondered how he'd feel about his mom going out with my dad.

Wow, how did my life suddenly get so complicated?

CHAPTER 20

Alex came over so we could get ready together. When she got there, she was practically vibrating, she was so excited. And who could blame her; she looked awesome in her new blue dress.

"You look great!" I said. "That dress is perfect for you."

She did a twirl. "Thanks, Li! So what are *you* wearing?" she asked.

I looked at the three outfits I'd laid out on my bed and sighed. I wasn't happy with any of them; one was too small, one was too pink, and the third one was . . . well . . . boring. "I don't know, what do you think?"

"I think you might have something better in your closet," she said.

"I agree," Bubby said.

"Yes," Prissy chimed in. "Definitely there must be something better in there."

I shook my head. "I wish. These are my only fancy outfits."

"Why don't you check," Alex said.

Knowing I wasn't going to find anything, but apparently needing to prove to my friend and a couple of old-lady ghosts that I didn't have anything better, I opened my closet. "See? There's nothing else in here . . ."

"Did you look in the back?" Alex asked at the same time as Bubby said, "Look in the back."

I parted the clothes with my arms and pushed them to the sides.

And that's when I saw it. I gasped then turned toward Alex. "Where did this come from?"

She shook her head. "Not me. Take it out."

I reached back into my closet and pulled out the beautiful silver dress I'd never seen before.

"We made it," Ms. Lafontaine said.

"What do you mean, *we* made it?"

Alex just grinned; it was obvious she knew what was going on. But she kept quiet, allowing Prissy to continue. "When we were sewing the dresses for the fashion show, we thought we'd surprise you."

"Do you love it?" Bubby asked.

"Love it? I *adore* it! Prissy, this design is perfect!"

"I'm so glad you love it," Prissy said. "But this isn't one of my designs. This is one of Dolly's creations."

I held the dress up and looked at it again. "Wow, she really is talented!"

"I agree," Prissy said. "And this dress is perfect for you."

Alex couldn't wait any longer for me to finish my conversation with the ghosts. "Put it on, Lilah!"

I didn't need any more encouragement than that to strip off my clothes and slip the dress over my head.

"Oh, Lilah," Bubby said. "It looks beautiful on you. You will be the best-looking girl at the dance."

"Thanks, Bubby," I said, looking at myself in my big mirror. Until I got to my bare feet. "But what about shoes?"

"Oh!" Alex said. "Look on the floor at the back— in a pink box."

Sure enough, there was a fuchsia shoe box that had never been there before. I held my breath as I took off the lid.

Silver shoes!

I jumped up and down a little. They were so perfect!

"I don't suppose we sewed these?"

Ms. Lafontaine laughed. "No, dear. Dolly bought these for you."

"Dolly bought those," Alex said, obviously unable

to hear what Prissy had already explained. "And then we got your dad to sneak them into your closet."

"Wow," I said, feeling a bit overwhelmed. "You did all this for me?"

Alex threw herself at me and gave me a big hug. "Of course we did!"

I hugged her back and then had a horrible thought: "Don't crush the dress!"

She stepped back and we both checked our outfits.

Whew, disaster averted.

I slipped on the shoes and then it was time to really get ready for the dance. Alex had brought over her makeup, and with the help of Bubby and Prissy, we managed to make each other up so we looked like movie stars, but without overdoing it. It's a fine line with makeup, you know.

Having fashionable ghosts around was pretty darn cool!

"Are you going to dance with Andy?" Alex asked as she fluffed up her hair.

Like she needed to bother asking. "Of course I am. Aren't you going to dance with Sean?" It sounded so grown up to be talking about our dates. Dates! We had dates!

"I don't know."

I stopped brushing my hair and looked at her in the mirror.

"What do you mean?"

She shrugged, but wouldn't look at me.

"Alex? What's up?"

"I'm not sure if I like him, that's all."

Alex totally liked him. Alex liked *all* boys. And there was that hand-touching incident, so I knew Sean was totally on her radar. She was fibbing, I could tell. And I said so.

Alex spritzed product on her hair, seeming to take a really long time to make sure every lock was in just the right place. I was about to say something when she finally blurted out, "Maybe I'm just scared, 'kay? Maybe he's going to try to kiss me."

Oh.

Kissing.

Okay, that was reason to be scared.

I very suddenly had the same fear—that Andy might want to kiss me. How had I not even thought about the possibility?

"Do you *want* him to kiss you?" I asked, not sure if I wanted Andy to kiss me. Oh, I wasn't fooling anyone; *of course* I wanted Andy to kiss me. But kissing is HUGE!

"I *think* I want Sean to kiss me," Alex said, looking into my eyes finally. "But I don't know what to do. What you see on the movies doesn't really prepare—"

"You girls are too young to be kissing," Bubby interrupted, speaking in *that tone*. The tone that reminded me she wasn't just a fun person to have around. She was also a grown-up authority figure.

"Bubby, please. We are trying to have a private conversation."

"What did she say?" Alex asked.

"She says we're too young to be kissing boys."

Alex's face told me she was maybe thinking the same thing.

"Please, Bubby," I said. "We're not getting engaged or anything. I won't even use tongue."

"Tongue?" Alex looked sick. "Why would anyone want to use tongue?"

"I don't know. I mean, saliva? *Ew.* Germs." Apparently, I was a bit of a germophobe like my dad.

"Yeah, saliva's gross. Why do people even bother to French kiss?"

"And why is it called French kissing, anyway?" I wondered aloud.

Alex shrugged. "The French must have invented it, like French fries and French toast."

It seemed reasonable enough. But still . . . *ew.*

We needed to draw a line. I said, "I think we need to be at least . . . fourteen before we use tongue. So just kissing, plain old kissing at the dance. That's it."

"Oy," said Alex, sounding a lot like my dead grandmother. "How are you so confident? Aren't you scared?"

"Scared" wasn't the right word. "Terrified" was more like it.

When we came downstairs, Dad was sitting on the sofa looking all handsome. His hair was brushed and lying flat and his (new) outfit looked very stylish. As I got into the room, I even noticed he smelled good.

"Wow, you look nice," I said.

He looked at me funny. No, he wasn't just *looking* at me funny, he was totally staring.

"Dad?"

"Yeah?"

"Why are you looking at me like that?"

"You have makeup on. And a dress. You look so . . . grown up."

I couldn't help but smile. "Thanks."

Although the way Dad was looking, I'm not so sure he meant it as a compliment. He stood up and walked over to me, glancing over at Alex.

"You look nice, Alex. Your hair is very . . . high."

Alex beamed. "Thanks, so do you, Mr. Bloom. And you smell awesome. You must have a hot date tonight."

I shot a look at Alex, one that said, "Shut up!" She knew about Dad and Andy's mom going out, but *he* wasn't supposed to know that *we* knew.

Dad blushed a little but didn't say anything. He

looked at me again. "Wow, kid, you look . . ." His eyes got all glassy.

"Dad, don't get all weird, please."

He shook his head and pursed his lips. "Sorry."

Dads can get so sentimental sometimes.

"Oh, I almost forgot . . ." He reached into his pants pocket and pulled out a cell phone. "I got you a new phone."

Of course, I hadn't had a phone since the lightning did mine in. I took it from him. "Thanks, Dad! Wow, this is a really cool one!"

"With unlimited texting."

I smiled and then threw my arms around my nerdy but still very cool father. "Thank you so much!"

He grunted when I squeezed him so hard. "Don't wrinkle the shirt, Lilah."

I let him go. "Sorry."

"I programmed all the important numbers into it. So if you want to leave the dance early, just call or text me and I'll come get you."

Like I would ruin his date. "You can just come get us at eight thirty like we talked about, Dad."

He nodded.

I looked over at Alex. "You ready to go?"

She looked ill, which meant she was. Kinda.

"Oh, Lilah," Bubby said. "I'd like to go to the dance with you, but your father . . ."

I couldn't exactly respond to my grandmother

right there in front of my dad, but I was glad she wouldn't be there at the dance, getting up in my business. No one needs their grandmother peeping in on their first romantic experience. I mean, there would be no French kissing, but still . . .

"Don't worry, Dora," Prissy said. "I'll go and keep an eye on her."

"Great, the next best thing," I said.

"What's that, Lilah?" Dad said as he grabbed his keys.

I blinked as I realized I'd spoken out loud. "Oh, uh, I said I forgot my earrings."

He frowned. "No, you didn't."

My right hand rose to my earlobe. "Oh, whoops. Duh."

Dad grinned. "You must be a little nervous about your first dance."

He was right about me being nervous. But it wasn't dancing I was nervous about.

CHAPTER 21

We walked into the gym right at seven. Most of the other seventh graders were already there. The girls were all on the one side of the gym huddled together and the boys were all up on the bleachers, not surprisingly, watching the girls. There were a few teachers scattered around. Most were talking, but Mr. Robertson was standing in the corner, rocking to the music. I wondered if he'd gotten his band back together yet.

"There's everyone," Alex said, grabbing my arm and leading me over to where Fiona, Tamsin, and Anita were standing. Sherise's family was out of town, so she couldn't make it to the dance. She'd been really bummed about missing it, especially when she found out Alex and I had dates, but we promised to fill her in on Monday.

"Hi," Tamsin said as we joined them.

"Sean and Andrew are up on the bleachers," Fiona said.

"Thanks," I said without turning. Leave it to a friend to scope out your guy before you arrive.

"You going to dance with him?" Fiona asked me.

I nodded.

She asked Alex the same question.

She also nodded.

"What about you?" Alex asked Fiona. "Are you going to dance with someone?"

Fiona scanned the crowd on the bleachers. "I don't know. Maybe Sam."

"Sam?" I asked. "Sam Alpers?"

All of us looked over at Sam to size him up. It was at that moment that Sam decided to not-so-covertly stick his finger up his nose.

"EWWWW!" we all said.

"Okay," Fiona said. "So Sam's out."

"Too bad the eighth graders aren't here," Tamsin said, obviously sad that Tyler wasn't there to dance with (not that she had a chance with him, but I wasn't about to tell her that). That's what you get for crushing on someone outside your grade, but I still felt bad for her. And after watching Sam, I understood the appeal of more mature eighth-grade boys.

"Hi, Lilah," a boy said from behind me.

I turned to face Andy. My heart jumped into my throat.

"Oh, hi, Andy."

He was smiling, but he didn't look really happy. Maybe he was as nervous as I felt.

"Want to dance?" he asked. A squeal erupted from behind me. I tried to ignore it.

I glanced over to the middle of the gym that was supposed to be the dance floor. Even though a really good fast song was playing, there were exactly zero people dancing.

"Are you sure?" I asked him.

He looked over his shoulder at the dance floor and then back at me. His face got all red. "Sure, why not."

I swallowed and fought the urge to look over at my friends. "Okay."

"Let's *all* dance," Alex said from behind me.

I exhaled in relief, knowing the girls would help take the pressure off me and Andy.

We got to the middle of the gym and Andy turned to face me. I felt a bit dizzy but tried my best not to pass out from nerves.

I mean, sure, I'd danced with my friends tons of times, but with a boy? In front of the whole seventh-grade class?

"You'll do fine," Prissy said, obviously picking up on my nerves.

"Thanks," I said.

"For what?" Andy asked.

"Uh . . . for asking me to dance." I started dancing, finding my rhythm—the song had a good beat, so it was easy.

Andy smiled. Then he started moving his feet in what I guess was supposed to be dancing. He wasn't very good, just moving his feet from side to side and not moving his arms at all.

I caught Alex's attention and gave her a look. She glanced over at Andy and shrugged. Then she puckered up her lips.

I almost died right there on the dance floor.

Horrified, I returned my attention to Andy.

"You're a good dancer," he said. "I guess I don't have very good rhythm."

"You're doing great," I said. Even though it was kind of a lie.

"He gets it from me," Mr. Finkel said suddenly. "I was never a good dancer either."

"Oh."

"What?" Andy asked.

"Um, your father says hi."

He blushed. "My dad's here?"

I nodded and wondered if his dad being here would eliminate the chance of us kissing. Probably.

I must say, I was kind of relieved.

But then, just as I was starting to enjoy myself, the song ended. Not the end of the world, right? There would be more songs.

But the next song that came on was a slow song. The kind that *couples* dance to. I looked over at Alex who gave me a very conspicuous thumbs-up.

"Do you want to keep dancing?" Andy asked, his voice cracking on the "keep."

I looked at him to gauge if he *wanted* to keep dancing. He looked like maybe he did. I nodded.

He put his hands on my waist, which felt strange.

I put my arms around his neck. Also strange. As we got closer, I noticed he smelled nice, like soap and fabric softener. "You smell good," I said.

"Thanks," he said. "You do, too."

Weird.

And then we were slow dancing, going around in circles on the dance floor. I pretended not to notice when he stepped on my foot, but then he mumbled a "sorry," so I had to tell him it was okay.

On the second turn around the gym, I noticed Alex dancing with Sean. I gave her a thumbs-up behind Andy's back. She smiled and seemed to pull Sean even closer to her.

I wondered if she was still nervous about kissing him. She sure didn't seem to be. If anything, *he* looked nervous and was dancing like he was tied to a board.

Another quarter turn had me facing Fiona who was (*gasp!*) dancing with digging-for-gold Sam. Well, she was moving to the music with her wrists on his shoulders, seeming to keep him as far away as possible.

Tamsin and Anita watched in horror from the sidelines.

I felt pretty lucky. I had my choice of guy who really seemed to like me. He was not a nose picker AND he smelled nice.

"I'm having a nice time," I said.

Andy leaned back so he could look at me. He smiled. "Me, too."

The way he was staring into my eyes kind of freaked me out. Time for a subject change. "So what do you think of my dad and your mom?"

He cocked his head. "What do you mean?"

Oh.

"They're out on a date right now."

He frowned. "With each other?"

Boys can be so clueless sometimes. "Yes, with each other. They sat together at the fashion show last night."

"That was your dad?" He seemed shocked.

"Yeah."

"Oh."

I got suddenly defensive. "What does that mean?"

The song ended and a fast one came on again. I didn't really feel like dancing, not while we were trying to have a conversation, anyway.

"Want to get a soda?" I asked.

Andy nodded, so we headed over to where Mr. Burrows was selling sodas from a cooler full of ice. "I'll buy yours," he said, pulling some bills out of his pocket.

"Thanks."

We took our sodas and went to sit on the bleachers, away from the crowds of boys.

"So what did you mean back there," I said. "About my dad?"

He popped open his soda can and took a long drink. I wondered if it was going to fizz up his nose. I could never have drunk that much without my nose fizzing up.

Finally, he turned to me and said, "It's not that it's your dad, I mean, he seemed pretty nice . . . it's just . . ."

"He's worried about me," Mr. Finkel said.

"You're worried about your dad, aren't you?"

Andy nodded, running his thumb around the lip of his soda can.

"He's okay with it, you know. With your mom dating, I mean."

He looked up at me, his face all scrunched up. "Really? Did he say that?"

Mr. Finkel jumped in. "I just want her to be happy."

I repeated it to Andy.

"He's not jealous?"

I opened my mouth to say no, but shut it when Mr. Finkel said, "I wish I could have spent more years with you and your mother, Son. But it wasn't to be. Your mom is lonely and Lilah's father is, too. They both deserve to be happy. I can't make your mom happy anymore."

I told Andy what his dad said. He looked like he was going to cry, so I asked him if he wanted to go outside to get some air.

He nodded, and we left the gym.

We sat down on the steps, so close that our thighs were touching.

"Thanks, Lilah," Andy said after a few quiet minutes.

"For what?"

He looked at me. "For everything. For the fundraiser, for telling me about my dad, for coming to the dance with me."

"You're welcome."

And then, before I knew it, Andy was holding my hand.

My brain emptied of all thoughts except *OH*

MY GOODNESS, ANDY FINKEL IS HOLDING MY HAND!

And then that was replaced by *OH MY GOODNESS, ANDY FINKEL IS KISSING ME!*

I suddenly realized I was staring at his closed eyelids, so I closed my own eyes and leaned a little closer.

Then it was over.

"I like you, Lilah," he said.

"Obviously. I like you, too, Andy."

He smiled. "Can I kiss you again?"

I nodded. "No tongue though, okay?"

He frowned. "Huh?"

"I have some rules. No tongue or saliva."

Even outside in the dusk I could tell his face was getting very red. I mean, it was embarrassing, but a girl has to lay down the law on these things.

"Just a regular kiss. Is that okay?"

"Yes. It's very okay." I squeezed his hand.

And then he kissed me again. This time, my one thought was, *Kissing is nice. Especially because it's with Andy Finkel.*

When the kiss was over, we kept holding hands. It felt nice, his fingers twined in mine.

"Is he a good kisser?" a voice said. It sounded a lot like Ms. Lafontaine.

"Yes, he *is* a good kisser," I said out loud, my eyes on Andy's.

He looked down. "Who's asking?"

"Don't worry, it's not your dad," I said. "But the answer would have been the same."

Andy and I were the last kids waiting outside the school after the dance was over. We sat on the steps after we'd said good-bye to all of our friends. (Alex got a lift with Fiona to give me and Andy some more alone time. She's really good that way. AND I think she was kind of happy to get away from Sean, who'd tried to kiss her using his tongue. Needless to say, they were *so* over.) It was almost nine o'clock, but I knew Dad and Andy's mom were both on their way because at 8:40, I had texted Dad with WHERE R U? and he texted back SRY IM ON MY WAY.

"They must be having a good time," I said to Andy. He was still holding my hand. That meant we were official.

"I guess," he said. I think he still wasn't sold on the idea of our parents dating, but I knew that once he really got to know my dad, he'd be okay with it. I mean, it was kind of weird because if our parents got married, we'd be stepbrother and stepsister, but I tried not to think about that.

Mr. Robertson came out of the school behind us. "Hey, kids, are you okay out here?"

I nodded, discreetly letting go of Andy's hand. "Our parents are coming, they're just a bit late."

"You sure?"

"Yep. Oh, there's my dad now." I pointed at the car pulling up to the school.

"And my mom's right behind," Andy said in a strange voice.

Mr. Robertson nodded. "Okay, have a great weekend!"

Andy and I both stood up. "C'mon and meet my dad," I said to Andy, resisting the urge to take his hand. I mean, I didn't need Dad having a coronary right there.

Dad got out of the car and Andy's mom got out of hers. It was kind of weird, but I worked quickly to try to diffuse the weirdness.

"Dad, this is Andy Finkel."

Dad glanced over at Andy's mom. I could tell he was trying to figure out what to do. But being the polite guy he is, he stuck his hand out toward Andy. "Hi, uh, Andy. Nice to meet you."

I held my breath, but then Andy shook my dad's hand like a pro. "Nice to meet you also, Mr. Bloom."

"Hi, honey," Mrs. Finkel said as she walked up to us. "And this must be Lilah?"

I looked from her to Dad, whose face was a little

green. I guess he forgot to tell Andy's mom that they were supposed to be dating on the down low.

"Hi, Mrs. Finkel."

"Please, call me Rachel."

She was really pretty up close. I could totally see why Dad was smitten. And he was. He was watching her with googly eyes. I wondered if they'd kissed on their date.

Ew. TMI.

"So we should get going, Dad," I said.

His head snapped toward me. "What's that, Lilah?"

I didn't laugh, but I wanted to. "I said we should go."

"Oh, right."

I turned to Andy. "I guess I'll see you on Monday."

"Actually," Rachel said, "the four of us are going to go out for dinner tomorrow night. If that's okay."

If that's okay? *Of course* it was okay. I sighed in relief. Finally one of Dad's dates went well!

"That would be great," I said. "I guess I'll see you tomorrow then, Andy."

He seemed happy about that. "Great, see you then."

Then he and his mom got in their car and Dad and I got in ours.

"So . . . ," I said.

He didn't say anything.

"Are you going to tell me about what just happened?" It was an open question that either my father or my dead grandmother were welcome to answer.

While Dad chewed on his lower lip and pulled the car from the curb, Bubby decided to fill me in.

"Oh, Lilah, it was wonderful. They got along so well from the second they sat down. And isn't she pretty? And she's smart, too. I'm so pleased!"

I tried not to smile, but it was hard. I was so happy that Dad finally met someone he really liked, AND it was Andy's mom!

"Dad?"

"Huh?"

"Come on, Dad. Obviously the *coffee with a friend* was with Andy's mom."

He glanced over. "I didn't want to make you feel awkward."

"I don't feel awkward at all. I think it's great."

After a few quiet moments, he said, "Thanks, kid."

"You like her, don't you?"

He did a double take at me, but then sighed. "Yeah, I think I do."

That was good enough for me.

And apparently my grandmother, too. "Lilah, thank you so much. I'm so proud of you for helping your father like this."

Which was kind of funny of her to say because I had nothing to do with this date at all, unless you count forcing him to go to the fashion show against his will. I guess that counts a little.

"So, Lilah," Dad said in his fatherly voice. I knew what was coming.

"Yeah?"

He cleared his throat. "You and Andy?"

"Yeah?" I knew what he was going to ask. He was going to ask if Andy and I were official. I figured there was no point lying, since we were putting all our cards on the table.

But instead he said, "Is he a good kisser?"

ACK! MY FATHER KNOWS ANDY KISSED ME!

I held my breath, not sure what to say. But the way dad glanced over and smirked, I figured it out.

"Yeah, but don't worry, he doesn't use his tongue."

Dad did another double take.

"Oy," said my grandmother.

"Oy," said my dad at the same time.

But it was all good. Yup, everything was very all good.

EPILOGUE

One day, a surprise FedEx envelope showed up, addressed to *me*. Inside were tickets and back-stage passes to the hottest concert of the year.

Dad said getting tickets like that meant we had to rent a limousine for the night. I wasn't about to argue; limousines are way cool.

The limo let us out in front of the stage door. I was so pumped that I could barely contain myself as I dragged Andy up to the huge security guy who stood guard at the door.

"Come on!"

"Lilah, we're coming," Alex said as she piled out of the limo, leaving only Dad and Andy's mom to climb out behind her. Dad and Rachel were our chaperones, but they were such a fun couple, it wasn't so bad.

I showed the security guy the badge that hung around my neck, and he checked my name against the list on his clipboard. He was pretty diligent about checking all of our badges, but in only a few minutes, he waved us all in. "You'll want the fifth door up on the right," he said as we filed past him.

I grabbed Andy's arm. "Do you believe we're here? This is SO cool!"

He peeled my fingers off him. "Ow, Lilah!"

"Oh, sorry! I'm just SO excited."

"I'm not sure why you're getting so worked up."

"Are you kidding me, Andy? This is *everything*. This is a dream come true."

He leaned down and gave me a quick kiss on my cheek, keeping his eyes on my dad. "Have I told you lately how incredibly cool you are, Lilah Bloom?"

I smiled up at him. "*You* are the epitome of cool, you know that, Andy Finkel?"

"Epitome? Good Scrabble word," he said. "Anyway, come on."

We got to the green room and I knocked hesitantly on the door. Even though we had the passes, it still felt odd.

The door opened into a room full of people.

"Uh, hi, I'm Lilah Bloom," I said, holding up

my badge and suddenly feeling a lot smaller than usual.

The man who'd opened the door stuck out his hand. "Phil Rivers, the band's producer. Nice to meet you, Lilah."

"Is that Lilah?" a voice yelled from the back of the room. And then before I knew it, I was being hugged by my music teacher. Excuse me, my *former* music teacher.

"Hi, Mr. Robertson," I said, my heart pounding with excitement.

"Oh, Lilah, I'm not your teacher anymore. You can call me Frankie."

It felt weird, but I nodded. "Okay, Frankie. Um, well, you know Andy and Alex." I pointed over my friends' heads. "And back there, that's my dad and Rachel, who's Andy's mom."

"Hi," he said, smiling at everyone in turn.

"Yeah, uh, thanks for the tickets," Andy said, sounding a bit funny. I wondered if he was starstruck all of a sudden.

Even *I* was totally starstruck!

Like the polite guy he was, Mr. Rob . . . Frankie invited everyone into the room and introduced us all to the band.

Right after that, I cornered him at the fridge. "I just wanted to thank you for the passes. You totally didn't have to do this. I mean, we really appreciate it, but when I opened the envelope . . ." My throat closed up around my words.

"Lilah," he said, putting his hand on my shoulder. "If it wasn't for you, Jet Black Wig wouldn't exist. You *made* this happen."

I looked down, fighting tears. You weren't supposed to bawl at a rock concert, and here I was on the verge of blubbering like a two-year-old.

"Lilah?" he said, his tone making me look up at him. "Did she ever come back to you? I would have thought she would have wanted to thank you."

I knew he meant Serena, his former bandmate and girlfriend, the one who had died.

I shook my head. "Sorry. Just the one time."

He didn't hide his disappointment, but nodded before he said, "How's everything going for you?"

I shrugged. "Okay, more or less. I mean, I hear dead people, but that's same-old, same-old for Lilah Bloom, right?"

He snorted. "You've got a great sense of humor, Lilah. I always thought you were something special."

"Yeah, and not an ounce of drumming talent."

"That's not true. I hope you've been practicing."

"Yeah, although I'm not sure what good it's doing."

"I'm sure it's doing a lot of good. Keep at it. Skill

doesn't come overnight, you know. So, what's the name of your band?"

"We're not exactly sure. Maybe Medium or Psychic Phenomenon. But I think we have lots of time to figure it out before we're actually good enough to play any gigs."

He gave me a huge smile. "Well I look forward to hearing about Medium or Psychic Phenomenon hitting it big. Please keep in touch, Lilah. Maybe down the road we can send you to Phil over there at Sony."

And he seemed to really mean it, too. I looked over at Phil and the rest of the band. "I should let you get back to them. You go on soon."

"Thanks again, Lilah. For everything." He gave me another hug. "And I hope the seats are okay."

"Uh, are you kidding, Mr. . . . Frankie? These are front row."

He smiled and handed me the drumsticks out of his back pocket. "Here. Keep these."

How cool is that? Frankie Robertson's drumsticks.

He turned to join his bandmates.

But there was one last thing. "Hey, Frankie?"

He turned back. "Yeah?"

"She's really proud, you know. I don't have to hear her say it to know it's true."

Frankie smiled and nodded before returning to the rest of Jet Black Wig.

The crowd screamed for the band to come out for a second encore. And I'm pretty sure my screams were the loudest. It wasn't even just because the drummer used to be my music teacher, either. The truth was Jet Black Wig was an awesome band.

It was no mystery why they were at the top of the charts and selling tons of records. And I had listened to their songs so many times, I knew every one by heart.

So when they came back out, picked up their instruments, and began to play, I was surprised to not recognize the tune as one of theirs.

The lead singer, Stella King (Serena's replacement), leaned into the mic as the guys behind her looped the opening bars of the song.

"We'd like to play a special song to end the show tonight," she said, her voice reverberating through the huge amps.

The crowd cheered.

"This song," Stella said as she strummed a chord on her guitar, "is by a little band called Oasis and it's called 'Lyla.'" She looked down into the audience right into my eyes. "And it's for you. Thank you, Lilah."

I swear, I almost passed out from the shock. I looked up at Frankie behind his drum kit, and he was looking right at me. He smiled and winked and then started drumming like the rock star he was.

Yeah, being a medium was going to be all right, after all.

ACKNOWLEDGMENTS

They say it takes a village to raise a child. Well, if that's true, this baby took an enormous metropolis to feed, change, discipline, educate, and dress to get it ready to go out in the world. It's been a long journey and I know I'm going to miss thanking people who helped shape me and this book, so if you are reading this and think you should have been mentioned here, but weren't, you're probably right; please accept my apologies AND my thanks.

My first thank-you goes to Lynda Simmons and Rachael Preston—two great authors and writing teachers who helped me realize even at the very beginning that maybe I could do this.

I've had the good fortune to have had many readers for this and my other works. Thank you for your honest feedback, encouragement, and support:

Christine Carleton, Sarah Goodhope, Amanda Morgan, Carrie Grosvenor, and Kay Chornook.

To the excellent writer friends who read, encouraged, picked me up and dusted me off, and have been endless founts of support, help, and love: Lisa McMann, Eileen Cook, A. S. (Amy) King, Robin Brande, Bev Katz Rosenbaum, Danielle Younge-Ullman, Maureen McGowan, Lauren Baratz-Logsted, and Jenny Gardiner. Thank you!

Thank you to Janet Reid for your ongoing support and education of writers. Cupcakes are always on me.

A big shout-out to the groups of which I'm a member—you are filled with awesome: The Debutante Ball (http://www.thedebutanteball.com), The Class of 2012 (www.classof2k12.com), The Apocalypsies (http://apocalypsies.blogspot.com), and Backspace (www.bksp.org).

Huge thank-you to the funny, encouraging, and eternally level-headed Michelle Humphrey. May there be an endless supply of mashed potato–topped cornbread cupcakes on your desk, even if I still think they're wrong.

To Margaret Miller goes another big thank-you, for seeing the diamond in the rough and taking a chance on me. Also thanks to Caroline Abbey, who took over this project and made the transition seamless. You've been awesome from the get-go and I so appreciate you! Thanks to the rest of the team at Bloomsbury Kids who made sure this book was not just readable, but beautiful and shiny and worthy of slipping under my pillow at night.

Thank you to my parents, Dan and Marcia Levy, for teaching me to love books and encouraging me to follow my dreams. And I would be remiss if I didn't thank my brothers for rounding out my rich childhood and providing almost endless material for future books.

And of course, I must thank my husband, Deke—Team Snow cocaptain. I love you more than every letter, comma, and period in this book.

And to the rest of the readers of this book—YOU—my friend, family member, or the person I may not yet know, but who plunked down your money to be entertained by the story I made up in my head: THANK YOU and I truly hope you enjoyed reading this book as much I enjoyed writing it.